Things Unknown to Lily

THE FIFTH IN A SERIES

SHERRY BOAS

Caritas Press, Arizona, USA

THINGS UNKNOWN TO LILY

Sherry Boas

First Edition

10 9 8 7 6 5 4 3 2 1

ISBN 978-1-940209-07-4

Cover photo: © denys_kuvaiev via Fotolia

For reorders and other works by Sherry Boas, visit CaritasPress.org

For Cindy, one of those rare friends who makes you stop—in the middle of the strife and suffering and confusion and laughter and joy of daily life—and say to yourself, "I don't know what I would do without her."

Contents

1

The Tunnel

Would it be wrong for me to wish I had never loved him? It is dark, and I can barely make out the contour of his cheek bone. If it wasn't for the silver light seeping through the organdy at the window, there would be no hope of seeing him at all. I drop my face closer to his to make out more detail, though I don't know why, since I've memorized everything there is to know about his face. You don't love a man as much as I love John without memorizing him. I do it not only out of love, but out of necessity. There will come a day when my memory is all I will have.

I hover at a safe distance, I hope, far enough that my breath will not fall on his cheek. I want to kiss him, but I resist, and I feel my lips move with a silent request. "Can't you just wake from this, John? Can't there be a new day?"

I met John on the day Delmuro died. These are two unrelated events, but there they are forever linked. I don't remember what I thought of John. The whole world was caught up in the shock and grief of losing another president.

John didn't ring the doorbell that day. Not much of a knock either. More of a tapping on the door. He didn't want the bell to startle me. It would have, too, because I'm sure I was deep in thought, and the doorbell always startles me, even if I am expecting it to ring. And so does the telephone or someone entering the room, even though I know full well I don't live alone and shouldn't be surprised to hear a voice. But my insides jump clear out of my outsides every time.

It's hereditary I suppose. Of all the memories I have of Mama and Daddy together, the clearest one is of her collapsed in his arms. He liked to sneak up behind her while her mind was on something else and grab her around the waist. She despised him for it. He finally stopped doing it the day he crept up and spoke into her hair while she was cutting potatoes. He had to catch her before she went to the ground, and it must have dawned on the both of them that she could have fallen on her knife. When she regained her senses, she pounded his chest as he offered profuse apologies, which she refused to accept. I didn't understand that then. And I don't now. I have never refused to accept an apology from John, as many as there have been.

John was there at my door that day to bring me something I thought I sorely needed. And if it wasn't for that "weakness," I would have never met him. Neediness can shape a future, in good and bad ways. To tell the truth, on a night like this one, I'm not sure which that was.

John lets out a small gasp in his sleep and then turns onto his side, facing away from me. I feel a loss again.

I don't know why I feel the need to keep vigil over him, but I will sit here until morning as he sleeps, unless I myself somehow succumb to sleep.

You probably want to ask me what happened, to make tonight such a bad one, and I would have to tell you the trouble is not based on the "what" but the "where." John lives in a dark place a solid thirty percent of the time, and I am a part-time resident there as well. Plus I spend another twenty percent fearing and waiting. Something in him believes he belongs in the dark, so he will retreat there. Because I love him, I go there too. I'm not free to leave it as long as he is there. It wouldn't be right to leave him there alone. Gone are the days when he will come with me into the light, just for the sake of coming with me. He is no longer that captivated by me.

The darkness is not just a lack of something, like what happens when you turn off the light in a room. The darkness is a thing of its own. I don't know what kind of thing it is. John won't tell me. But I have surmised from the few words he has spoken on the subject, that he is living with a deep regret, which now and then, and at an increasing rate, consumes him. And when it does, it is like entering a long dark tunnel, clinging to the walls, our cheeks and palms pressed against the cold concrete, moving forward by bits, not knowing when or if we will see that pinprick of light.

We thought getting out of Seattle would help. So we traded the gray veiled skies for one of the sunniest places in the world— Phoenix, Arizona. Did I say, "*we* thought?" Let me rephrase that. John did not think we were moving here for his condition. He thought we were moving for mine. I was tired of walking in the rain, wondering when my feet were going to fly out from under me. Walking on a sidewalk you can't see is hard enough, but a wet one is just that much harder.

Despite the boost in Serotonin that I'm sure 365 days of sunshine ensures, I see now that Arizona might not have been such a good idea. It was a trade-off, moving away from family, especially family like my in-laws. I have to say, my first taste of familial love was a long time coming, and it felt really good. I don't know how I managed without it all my life. I don't know how I'm not crazy for the lack of it in my early days, but I can honestly tell you I knew nothing or little of it for the first twenty-seven years of my life. The Lovelys have ruined me. If I had to live without it now, I would indeed go insane.

That is, if I wasn't already insane from a host of other things that have deprived me of my sanity, not the least of which are my own eyes. My vision continues to decline, at a faster rate than they had predicted, and if it keeps on, I will be completely blind by the time I am thirty-five. My severe nearsightedness is caused by my extremely elongated eyeball, which has resulted in tears in my macula and bleeding beneath the retina. I don't know why it is progressing so quickly. I've tried to take care of my eyes. I've babied them, really. When I was a kid, I was excused from P.E. because any blow to the eye, or even a slight jar could have detached one of my retinas. Mama would not even allow me to skip rope or jog. "You don't need to be jarring those eyeballs," she'd say. "There ain't no thicker Coke bottles than you're already wearin' and we can't afford to keep getting you new ones every six months."

Actually, there always are ever-thicker Coke bottles. Unfortunately, no matter how thick they make them now, it won't do me any good. Simply and sorrowfully put, I've got the kind of eyes that can't be fixed.

So, you can see why I am putting off telling John what I should have told him weeks ago. I am the self-appointed human shield between John and all unpleasant realities, so it's always difficult when I have to be the one to send him into the darkness. I will have to find the right time. I hope it comes soon.

In his optimistic moments, John paints pretty pictures of what we're going to squeeze in while I can still see. We'll travel and maybe even live in Ireland part of the year. I fear if I told him that may never come to pass, whatever light he finds in that thought would get swallowed up by the swine in the pit. Some people don't believe such places exist this side of hell, but the pit is a very real thing. I have to admit, I once could have been convinced those places are too far away to warrant my concern. Not anymore. I will no longer argue that light is always the victor over darkness, though I still agree it is a nice thought.

I really don't know what God was thinking, matching up a woman who is going blind with a man who spirals into depression for much lesser reasons than a blind wife. But one thing I know for sure about John is that he is devoted to me. If I have memorized every curve and angle of his face, he has memorized every pore in mine. Never will I have to worry what will happen to me when I can no longer do certain things for myself. He has attended to my every need and the vast majority of my wants since the moment he pledged his life to me. The vows he made to me are like one long continuous thread connecting one day to the next. He is living them out in a way that I am sure must be foreign to most people who claim to be in love.

To hear him tell it, we owe "us" to his aunt Lily. Of all the people in the Lovely family, I feel I know Lily best, though I have never met her. I have heard all the stories. I have heard some of them from John, but mostly from a variety of other family members. There are times when it feels to me like John tries to avoid the topic of Lily altogether. I don't know why he would do that, but when he is in his darkest place, he doesn't allow Lily in. One time I tried to bring him out with a story Terry always tells about Lily's escapades on her two-wheeler, when she first learned to ride without training wheels.

"I never found those stories very funny," John said. "I always thought that was really bad judgment on someone's part letting her ride around like that. Could have been really dangerous."

From what I can tell, it was mostly just adventurous. And maybe a little fattening. There was the day, when Lily was thirteen, and Bev got the call from grocery store security that her daughter had been nabbed for shoplifting.

Bev was finding it hard to comprehend. It had to be someone else's daughter. Both of hers were accounted for. Terry was sitting on the couch right in front of her reading the latest issue of *Modern Teen*. Lily was sulking in her room. Or *was* she? Bev shot down the hall, flung open Lily's door and found the room empty. Still, how could Lily be at the grocery store nearly two miles away? She wasn't exactly a swift walker, and forget jogging. And how would the grocery store get Bev's phone number? Lily was still unable to remember more than four numbers at a time. As these thoughts barraged Bev's brain, her tongue lay dormant.

"Hello? Ma'am?"

"Uhm yes, I'm sorry. What did she steal?"

The one word answer that followed put to rest all doubt about the identity of the shoplifter.

"Butter."

"Yup. That's my Lily. Is she OK?"

"She's fine. And I'm sure she didn't mean to steal. She just stuck three pounds of butter in her purse and walked out, waving and smiling at me as I followed her out to her bike. We're not going to press charges, of course. We just didn't know if you had authorized this little shopping excursion, and we wanted to keep her safe. Martha over in bakery recognized her. She was resourceful enough to find your phone number among the past custom birthday cake orders. That was real sleuthing. I think the ol' gal may be after my job." He chuckled for much longer than his wit warranted.

"Did you say 'her bike?'"

"Yes, ma'am. A right pretty pink bike with pearlized handle bars and purple streamers."

"Good gracious. I'm very sorry for all the trouble, Mr. uh—"

"You can call me Norbert."

"Norbert. I'm very sorry and I'll be right over to pick her up. You won't let her leave now, will you? She's not supposed to be out on that bike alone."

"Of course, of course. That's what we figured. She'll be right here with me. Don't you worry. She's with Martha right now. She walked her back to put away the butter, but I won't take my eyes off her until you get here, Mrs. Greeley."

"Thank you, Norbert. Thank you."

"Lily, a butter thief!" Terry exclaimed when Bev got off the phone. "Shocking. And yet, not."

"You coming with me?" asked Bev, picking her keys off the hook in the hallway.

"Oh yeah. I wouldn't miss this."

Terry had been following the butter saga for days. She had warned Bev that she better get to the store. The Greeley house had been three days without. On the first day, Lily accepted her ill fate with only a mild complaint and ate mayonnaise on her breakfast toast. On the second day, she protested loudly before spreading her mayo. On the third day, she ran screaming from the kitchen and went off to sulk, it was assumed, in her room. Only now, it was revealed, Lily decided to take matters into her own hands. She snuck off into the garage, put on her Union Jack bike helmet and off she went, obeying enough traffic laws along the busy four-lane street to get her to the store unscathed.

When Bev and Terry arrived to pick Lily up, she had a small paper bag in her arms.

"Lily," Bev hugged her and the bag crunched between them. "Don't ever go off again by yourself. That could have been very dangerous."

"But I get butter. You no buy me butter."

"How did you buy this? You don't have any money."

"It a present."

"No, Lily," Bev said. "You can't keep the butter. You didn't pay for it."

"Oh, it's OK," the security guard winked. "It's on me. I paid the cashier. It's just a pound."

"That's very kind of you, Norbert, but we don't want to reward Lily for stealing. I'm afraid she won't be able to take home the butter she came for."

"Oh, Auntie Bev, no," Terry pleaded. "We're all going to be miserable."

"Well, I guess your mama is right, Lily," Norbert said, accepting the bag of butter back into his large leathery hands. "But I'm sure you'll have your butter real soon if you promise never to go to the store without your mama again. Maybe she'll even bring you back tomorrow and buy you some."

Actually, Lily had to wait a week. Bev wanted to be certain the lesson was well learned. It's difficult to say if those seven days were harder on Lily or the people living with Lily. But she never did ride her bike to steal butter again. Every time she went shopping with Bev, Lily tried to stack four or five boxes of butter in the cart. After a series of intense negotiations, she usually ended up with two.

It is unclear whether the week without butter left any scars, but Lily did carry with her into adulthood a deep compassion for those deprived of their favorite foods. Sometimes when John was little, he would get sent to clean his room while everyone ate dessert. This would happen on the days he refused to pick up his toys before dinner. Sometimes it was his favorite dessert – colossal chocolate chunk peanut butter cookies. Lily would tuck her cookie into her purse and carry it upstairs to John. She'd find him there, crying in the middle of his toy-strewn floor. She'd sit with him and smile, as he ate the two halves of the cookie. He'd always break it and offer her one, and she would refuse.

I think I understand what John and Lily had. I have a beloved aunt myself. She was the one person in my life who didn't treat me like a curse. She treated me like I was something good that happened to her. And that has made a difference in the entirety of my thirty-two years on this earth. Whenever I'm feeling worthless, I remember Aunt Winnie. Her name was Winifred, actually, but no one ever called her that except my mama, who despised her for her decency. Where I come from, people have strange and often homely names, though the people are not homely. Not at all. Though they are, I must admit, very often a little strange. Not so much strange in mannerism or strange in how they present themselves. Just strange in how they think. My grandmother used to bury a potato in the back yard to kill a wart on someone's foot. By the time the potato sprouts, the wart is gone. Sometimes, even if the potato never sprouts, the wart goes away. My uncle once had nine small warts on his big toe and my grandmother planted nine potatoes, which amounted to nearly three pounds of potato. It might have worked, my grandmother insisted, if a stray dog hadn't dug them up, "for no other reason but to dig and cause misery." My uncle ended up having to go to a podiatrist to have the warts removed. It cost $475 and quite a lot of discomfort. Henceforth that dog was referred to as "that four-legged potato digger" and was assumed to be in cahoots with the foot doctor, who must have trained him to roam the neighborhood digging up potatoes, since potatoes are not something a dog would ordinarily dig up, according to my grandmother, who fancied herself an expert in many things, including dog behavior, human nature and wart removal. It was also said she could shoot an acorn out of a squirrel's hand and leave all the squirrel's fingers intact. Not that she would have had any qualms about shooting the squirrel. Would have been dinner that night for somebody. She had eight children, and they all wanted to eat three times a day.

My mama held grudges against the universe, particularly when it came to the circumstances of her upbringing. She hated that she grew up poor. Though she didn't remain truly poor in adulthood, she never discarded the baggage of poverty nor did she find a way to keep it safely stowed in the overhead compartment. I remember her buying four or five varieties of bread every time we went to the grocery store. We ended up having to rip it up and make bread pudding twice a week or feed it to the ducks. One day, after we had asked for something we weren't going to get, she lectured us on how good we had it. 'When I was a kid, we couldn't even afford to buy bread. We had to eat what my mama made. Ol' ugly bread I'd take in my lunch box while all the other kids had nice store-bought bread for their sandwiches."

It was hard to feel sorry for someone who was forced to eat homemade bread.

I lie thinking about all this as I stare into John's face. He rustles the covers and turns over, so I would see nothing but the back of his head, if I could indeed see. I am anxious for the night to be over. When morning comes, I will make myself a cup of coffee and some toast out of a pretty piece of store-bought bread and try to get up the courage to tell John the secret I have been keeping for far too long.

2

Favorite Aunts

Aunt Winnie was the sister of my father who ran away when we were four, five and six years old. He was an obliging down-home southerner with sun-weathered skin stretched over sharp facial bones. He had two distinct lengths of thick, wavy hair—short to the ears, long behind them—and a very small rear end, packed tightly into a pair of Wranglers, which he wore with tobacco-spattered, camel-colored work boots from Walmart, though he rarely had work. He was both red and blue. That was the joke. He spent my grandmother's disability check on Pabst Blue Ribbon and Marlboro Reds, both of which he partook of daily, in liberal quantities. He had met my midwestern barrel-racing mama at a rodeo when he was twenty-seven and she was nineteen and moved her out to Louisiana, which she hated, but never thought to move back home, even after Daddy left and granny died of emphysema. Mama resented her children for ruining her barrel-racing career and her figure and making her re-career into day care management. As we got older, we began to question why someone who disliked her own kids so much would choose to spend her days with children. Wouldn't it have been better for her to clean office buildings after everyone had gone home? Or do data processing in a cubicle by herself? Bill collecting? She would have been wildly successful at that one. I, for one, would write that check and have it posted before you could say "look away, Dixie Land," if I had her on the other end of the phone line.

We all understood why Daddy left. We just wished he had taken us with him. He had pet names for each of us (Rooster, Dimples and Speck) and gave us hugs and tousled our hair and would sit us on his knee after he'd had a number of beers and tell us stories about bears in campsites making people poop their pants. Between his slurred-speech stories, he would play the harmonica. And he was pretty darn good at it, we thought, but the best thing was how he took requests. Whatever we wanted him to play, he would play, giving preference to the suggestions of the youngest. When my aunt came to visit, she would try to stump him. But she never got too fancy with her song requests, always keeping it to selections that he would have had an occasion to encounter. In other words, not Vivaldi or anything.

My aunt had a lot of wisdom, which she shared through axioms and idioms coined by deep south philosophers. She never abandoned them, regardless of where her travels led. In fact, they probably became more meaningful because no one really understands them until a certain amount of life experience is acquired. Many of them had to do with men. For instance, "You never really know the length of a snake 'til he's dead and you can stretch eem out and measure eem." What that meant, exactly, was never clear to me until I started dating. Then, I understood that men are snakes, and you don't know how much misery you're in for until you've made your commitment.

Men are also water, as in "still water runs deep." That's what you say if a man is quiet and you never really know what he is thinking.

"A barking dog don't bite," is for those men who seem aggressive, but are really quite passive.

"You get used to hanging if you hang there long enough." This means you will eventually grow accustomed to being treated bad.

None of these have applied to John, but knowing my daddy, and other men like him all through my growing up, I can see why these sayings have survived the handing down through the generations. They let a woman know she is not alone—that the man she loves is just like any other, and she's not going to get anything better by scrapping everything and starting over again. My daddy was actually a good catch for my mama, if he could have stayed caught.

"Have you ever thought about trying to find your father?" John asks me as he sets my coffee cup in front of me, handle facing right, so I can grab it with my right hand. For some reason, we have gotten on the topic of my childhood instead of the one we really need to be discussing. This is one of those mornings when I try to make conversation to fill up the air. And one of those mornings when John will only break silence to give advice about other people's lives.

"Oh, I know where to find him," I say. "I just don't care to." I actually don't know, but I would be able to guess where to begin looking.

"You know, things aren't always as they seem. You might find him to be much different than you think. Years gone by can do that."

"I just don't have a desire to find out."

"Finding Pablo was one of the best things our family ever did for Lily. And for the rest of us too. Maybe it could be like that with your father."

"I don't know."

"I mean, he wasn't an abusive man, was he?"

"No."

"So people grow up, and they change. And they live with regrets."

I give this a lot more thought than I let John know. I don't want any pressure about it. But part of me would like to have a hug from my daddy. I know he would squeeze me tight until I could barely breathe and tell me how much he missed me. He would probably offer me a beer and tell me stories about the last twenty-five years. He, no doubt, has a number of other children by now. I would guess he stayed in touch with at least one or two of them. He probably found a woman who would let him sleep late and flick his ashes in the philodendron. My mama could flick ashes where she pleased, but my daddy caught hell for what he insisted was his contribution to fertilizing the plant. Mama also did not like that he spit tobacco in his empty beer can since she might accidentally pick it up and drink it one day, even though she never drank Pabst. My mama and daddy each had their own brand of cigarettes and beer. And come to think of it, toothpaste too.

"I can't stomach that stuff your daddy uses," she would say. "Tastes like floor polish."

"Yeah, you could probably give the floor a right nice shine, Buttercup," he'd retort. "Why don't you give it a try? Might as well spiffy the place up."

He'd call her Buttercup without a hint of sarcasm or irony in his tone. She hated it because she knew she was no buttercup, and she knew he knew she was no buttercup.

This kind of humor, the mark of a man who could not be controlled by any woman, lit something torrid and unquenchable inside my mama. Her fury would burn her on the inside and she would store up the combustion and release it on one of us kids sometime in the next twenty-four hour period. That's why, as much as we enjoyed his company and his humor, we were somewhat relieved when he was not around.

The thing is, my daddy always seemed happy. We never knew how he did it. And it perplexed and annoyed my mama too. His unfailing and mindless joviality. I have to admit, it annoyed me too as I got older and looked back on it. I wondered why he never got mad at her, never stood up for us. Never put his foot down and put her in her place. But now I understand. It would have done harm and not good. There was no effective way to change my mama. So my father just found his own method of keeping a very fragile peace from crashing to the floor in a thousand irreparable shards. Apparently, his method didn't work overly well, as he did end up leaving us. But that was due to a flaw in character, a moral deficit, I am sure of it. I have had fleeting thoughts of leaving John, and I willfully knock them out of my head. I know that would be wrong, and I won't entertain it. But my father didn't have that kind of moral code. He had a stunted conscience. He also didn't live with someone like John. John is a good man who suffers from bouts of depression. My mama (God rest her soul) was a bear to live with all the time. That she suffered from clinical depression, I have no doubt. But she also suffered from clinical meanness, if there would be such a thing.

I picture finding my father in a double-wide in some warm climate, his glistening grey whiskers pushing through his thick, tanned skin. He would be snapping a towel at the well-rounded rump of his latest love interest, a southern lady well into her sixties, dressed in tight-fitting jeans with forget-me-nots embroidered on the pockets and a pink eyelet blouse tied at the waist, not a strand of her large, teased, aberrant-red hairdo out of place and not one nick in her long hot-pink fingernails. She would be laughing at his playfulness and trying to snatch the towel away as he pulls her into his lap and kisses her on the cheek. He is truly fond of her, and she is wild about him, but you know it's not going to last. It never can with a man like him. He will always have another woman interested in him, and he will never have any self control.

That is how I picture my father.

I wonder what Lily thought she'd find in Pablo. And I wonder how accurate she was. She wouldn't have had any expectations. Just love. I don't even know if I can expect that of my father. The funny thing is, I always did believe he loved me. It was my mama who I thought didn't. I don't know how I came to the conclusion that the parent who left loved us, while the parent who stayed couldn't care less about us. I guess she would have found no occasion to yell and criticize if she didn't care how we turned out. Why she cared is the next question. I'm sure it all tied back into making a good impression or making her life easier in some way. If you can control everyone, and you've got them all afraid, you can save yourself time and labor. But the long and short of it was, shouting or no shouting, door slamming or no door slamming, she was the one who stayed and took care of us. Maybe not in the most gentle and loving way. But she was not the absent one. That should count for something.

I think we kind of glamorized my father's aura or whatever it is that is left behind when a person flees. There were certainly no remnants of his psyche or his conscience or the part of a person that allows him to make a total gift of himself to another human being. None of that ever did exist. We just had the story teller. Entertainers are wonderful people, but eventually you realize you need daily love, not memories of laughter you once had in sporadic doses. Just daily love. That's what you need.

3

Daisy Grace

I offered Marty and Annabel a ride. I don't know what I would have done if they had said yes. John would give you his last nickel plus the shirt off his back, but don't ask him to pick you up at the airport. All those converging and diverging lanes, signs coming at you too fast to read, traffic from behind riding your tail and then darting past like shooting stars in your side view mirrors. John once had to circle the airport three times before catching the exit that led to the parking garage of terminal two. He vowed then never again. "I will pay for their taxi ride, their shuttle or even their limousine," he would say, "but I will never pick anyone up at the airport." Thankfully, Annabel and Marty rented a car.

I answer the door to three people instead of two — a pair of large ones on each side of a small one. Although I can't see facial features, I can tell Annabel is tired. I don't know how exactly I know. Maybe you could call it a sixth sense, but it's probably more scientific than that. Maybe the angle of her shoulders. I am pretty sure the three of them are holding hands. I imagine Marty having a peaceful look about him, and a soft smile. In between them is an explosion of color, so I am able to surmise, or at least theorize, or at the very least imagine, that I am looking at a very dark skinned little girl whose hair is woven into a couple dozen braids tied in loops with orange, yellow and turquoise bows to match a sundress printed with large magnolias on a lime-green background. As my vision has gotten fuzzier, my mind has gotten sharper, it seems, and it has gotten good at filling in the blanks. The things I can't see with my retina, I can see with my mind's eye, and that is somewhat satisfying, usually. Though at this moment, I crave to see more. I kneel to look close into the girl's face. The child is probably the darkest-skinned person I have ever met.

"Oh my lans," I say. "Who is this beautiful young lady?"

"This is Daisy," Annabel says, and now I realize I was wrong about her fatigue, or maybe it just suddenly gave way to quiet jubilation, if jubilation can be quiet. "Daisy, this is your cousin Charlotte. Give her a hug."

The girl grabs me around the neck like we are age-old friends.

"My, my, you are pretty as a picture," I say, looking into her face after she finally releases my neck. "So, this beautiful girl is my cousin?"

"That's right. We met her in Jamaica. It all becomes final early next year, but she has been with us for a little over a month now."

"Well, congratulations," I stand and hug Annabel and then Marty. "Well look at you, handsome. How are you, Honey? It's been since the wedding, and I do feel awful for not keeping better touch with you two."

"Well, that's how life goes," Marty says. "Fast."

"Sometimes fast and furious," Annabel says. "We have been keeping this news for a surprise."

"Well, I've got to hear all about it. Come on in and sit down.

I just made some sweet tea. And I've got some ginger snaps. Do you like cookies, Daisy?"

I hear no answer so I imagine she is looking up at Annabel for an answer.

"Oh, she's a cookie monster," Marty says.

Annabel follows me into the kitchen. "Where's John?"

"Oh, he'll be back in a minute. He just ran to the store." John needed to pick up his prescription refill, and for some reason, waited until it was time for our guests to arrive. I say "for some reason," but I know the reason. It is typical of him when he is in the dark.

Marty takes Daisy out on the back porch to see my collection of wind chimes, which are kicking up quite a fuss. It's always windy in the desert. I know because I wear hats. And hats have been difficult for me to keep on my head since we moved out here.

"How is John?" Annabel asks as she puts ice cubes into a pitcher.

"He's fine," I pour tea over the ice. "He should be back soon."

"But how is he? How is he really?"

"I don't know Annabel." I stir the tea.

"It's OK, Charlotte. You can tell me. I've known about his depression for a long time. Aunt Terry told me she is really worried about him."

"She is?"

"She didn't tell you?" Annabel swirls the tea, and the ice clunks against the pitcher. Shes got a pretty good technique for a Yankee.

"Tell me what?"

"That she is worried?"

"No. She probably thinks I worry enough already."

"Probably."

"We don't really talk about it." I pour four glasses of tea, hoping I got them all somewhere close to the top. "I don't want to talk about my own husband behind his back.'

"No. I know. But at some point, you've got to ask for help if you need it." She takes a sip from one of the glasses. "Boy, that's good tea."

"I just don't understand what's at the root of it. If I knew that, I might be able to help him. I mean, sometimes I wonder. Is it me? Is it my condition? Is he depressed over being stuck with me?"

"Oh, Charlotte, that's nonsense. John thinks the world of you. He struggled with this long before he knew you. In fact, he wasn't ever going to get married because he didn't want to drag anyone else into his misery."

This does not surprise me. I wasn't sure if he would ever acknowledge there was something romantic brewing between us. I know he never intended to fall in love with me—or anyone. That's what he told me on the day he proposed. It went something like this:

"I hesitate to tell you I don't want to go through life without you, Charlotte."

"Why hesitate?"

"Because it sounds like a proposal."

"A proposal? What kind of proposal?"

"One of marriage."

"And it's not?"

"No."

"Then I can see why you wouldn't want to tell me that. Because that's how I would have interpreted it."

"Well, it's not that I *wouldn't* want to marry you."

"It's not?"

"No."

"So, you *would* want to marry me?"

"I would. Yes. But I can't."

"Why?"

"I wouldn't want to do that to you?"

"Do what?"

"Get you stuck with me the rest of your life."

"How could that be a bad thing?"

"It could be. I struggle, Charlotte."

"Struggle with what?"

"Some very bad days."

"Don't we all?"

"But my bad days are very dark."

"You are trying to tell me that you suffer from depression."

"Yes."

"Well, I suffer from blindness. We all suffer from something, John. And I don't want to live my life without you either."

And so, we got married.

In the times when the depression is at bay, John is very romantic. Not in the dimming the lights and pouring glasses of wine kind of way, but in a sweet, "totally into the other" kind of way. In those time, he never lets me forget that I am his beloved bride. He studies the wave in my hair and runs his fingers along my hairline and then asks me if I want him to read to me. I always say yes. He asks me what and I tell him one of three things: *David Copperfield*, *The Divine Comedy*, or *Song of Songs*. I most often request *Song of Songs* because the writer of that book captures everything I felt for John when I first fell in love with him, and I can feel it all over again when he reads to me. The bride has been marred, burned by the sun because she was forced into servitude, but she is still beautiful because the Bridegroom loves her. I used to wonder who on earth could ever fall in love with me. And after John did, I started believing everything he said about me. I started believing that the admiration in his eyes must have been a result of something admirable, and I started feeling the way he saw me—beautiful. I understood things about myself I had never known existed. Lovely things. I am sad to say that when he is in his depression, I question all those things or forget about them altogether. I regret—no, I grieve—that I haven't been able to remain, as the Bridegroom sees the Bride.

Like a lily among thorns, so are you among the maidens, my darling.

"I think I just take it all too personally," I tell Annabel. "I feel like my love should be enough to make him happy."

"If only curing people's hurts could be that easy," Annabel says.

"Isn't love supposed to fix everything?"

"Maybe not in the short term. Has he gotten worse?"

"It feels to me like he has. But who's to say I am able to see things the way they really are."

"We'll get him some help."

"He won't take it."

"I know you're right. In the darkest times, he won't agree. And in the times when the darkness lifts, he doesn't feel compelled to fix anything. It's like the leaky roof."

"Yep. So tell me the story of Daisy."

"The story of Daisy. Well that's a story that starts long ago."

Annabel had just met Marty when he invited her to accompany him on a mission to serve the disabled and impoverished people of Kingston, Jamaica. They suffered profound losses and profound gains there, back when they barely knew each other. Those were the ties that swiftly bound them together. After they were married, they returned to the Kingston mission every year to work during their vacation.

While Annabel had gone there the first time to escape the

tough decision of which man to marry (neither of whom was Marty), all the times after that, she was running *to* something, not *away* from it.

On their initial return, one of the first people they saw was Bennie, who was still wearing the cat watch Annabel gave him. The formerly mute man had some extremely happy news for them. For some inexplicable reason, it was Annabel who inspired Bennie to talk on that very first visit to the mission. Something about her and that cat watch she wore touched something in him and made him remember the desire to talk. After she and Marty left, Bennie kept talking. One day, he was able to tell the people who run the mission of his desire to find his mother and directions as to where she might be found.

She was lying in a dirt-floor shack, consumed by feelings of intense guilt for having left her son at the mission home those many years ago, though there was no way she could have taken care of him. She was destitute and ill and saw no other choice but to give him up to the "good Fathers" at the home. But her decision so haunted her that she assumed her arthritis and every other illness, ailment and misery that came her way was her punishment for "abandoning" Bennie. She was unable to leave her shack and survived only by the kindness of neighbors who brought her food whenever they could. Most of the time, she didn't care if they did or didn't. She had long ago lost her will to live, but it was hard not to appease her hunger when there was food right before her. She would have given it away, but she had no way of bringing it anywhere. And she couldn't let something so scarce and precious go to waste. Every day that she awoke, she was devastated that she was still alive. She had hoped and wished and prayed to die. And then one day she opened her eyes, and there was Bennie, standing over her. She thought she had died and she was being smiled on by an angel. It was only a few seconds before she recognized the strapping young man as her boy, though he no longer resembled a boy in any way, except his wide smile. He picked the old woman up off her tattered mat and carried her to the old sputtering paint-dinged jeep that Fr. Julian had received by donation and used to save souls from squalor. Fr. Julian drove while Bennie sat in the back, holding his mother on his lap, making promises that they would take care of her and get her a doctor and a soft bed and at least a couple of meals a day. A smile grew across her face as she thought maybe there might be some medicine to relieve her pain. But they could have kept the aspirin and the porridge, because what she wanted most, of course, was to be with Bennie.

Nearly every day after that, he'd come to the home for women, where she was staying, and eat with her. He always said the food was better at the home for women than the home for men. While no food critic would have given either of them a favorable review, there was never a complaint about the fare at either house.

Bennie's mother kissed Annabel's hand when she met her. Then, Father Julian took Marty and Annabel to a new home opened and run by Poor Clare Sisters, who had relocated to the island as a result of fasting, prayer and good deal of persuasion on Father Julian's part.

"I was really blown away by what I saw there," Annabel tells me as she pours herself another glass of tea. "There was so much joy. All the children were happy to be with the sisters and each other. But there was one place where that joy was in particularly high concentration. There was almost this visible bright light emanating from this one child, and I was drawn to her as she sat there drawing or coloring, I couldn't tell because her back was to me. I couldn't even see her face, so I didn't know what was so special about her. As I got closer I saw that she was tracing letter D's. Someone had drawn them in yellow highlighter, and she was tracing over them with pencil. Her tongue rested between her lips as she followed each line slowly and methodically. Sister Cecilia introduced her as Daisy Grace. She was a tiny thing, with thin arms and two braids, and when she looked in my eyes and smiled at me, my heart soared. I can't tell you why, but it was like I had found joy right there, embodied in one little person. Before I knew it, Marty and I were filling out adoption papers."

"You weren't planning to adopt a child when you went?" I asked Annabel.

"No, not planning that at all."

I remember fantasizing about my aunt adopting me someday. I didn't want anything bad to happen to Mama, so I always felt guilty for wishing to be orphaned. But how my childhood could have been different if I could have spent it with Aunt Winnie. I'll bet there would have been days when we spent the entire day in our pajamas watching *Hee Haw* reruns. We would have run to the store between episodes, with curlers in our hair, to get marshmallow pinwheels and Orange Crush. That night, we would have gotten all dressed up and gone into the city to see a play downtown. Maybe stop in at the art museum to see the latest exhibit. Aunt Winnie would have described every piece to me in painstaking detail, making it come alive in my head. She was very descriptive. She had a gift for words, but also for vision. No one else saw things quite like she did.

"Daisy Grace," I say. "That is such an adorable name."

"Her mother gave her the name Daisy. The sisters gave her Grace."

"It fits her."

"It does."

"Oh, sounds like John's home," I say, and then the garage door growls open.

John comes in all smiles and grabs Annabel into his arms, laughing, and, I imagine, hugging her so tight, he lifts her feet from the ground.

John and Annabel have been very close, but particularly in the last few years. Each credits the other with changing the future through a conversation they had about marriage. Annabel told John he would get married when he found the woman who understood that some things are worth suffering for. And he told her a number of things she couldn't quite understand until Marty.

"How's Boston?" John asks.

"Boston is cold."

"That's kind of how I imagined it."

"I've got a little surprise for you, John," Annabel says. And as if on cue, Marty brings Daisy in and gives John's hand a hearty shake. I can tell because the shock waves jostle John's voice in his chest.

"Hey, Marty, good to see you, man. Well now, look at this. This beautiful young lady wouldn't be the surprise now would she?"

"Yeah," Marty says. I imagine him beaming. "This is Daisy Grace, our daughter."

"Look at those beautiful eyes," John says softly. "She has Down syndrome, doesn't she?"

Well, how about that. Daisy and Lily share more in common than being named for flowers.

We all settle into soft furniture after dinner, except for John who assures us he'll join us after he finishes scraping the dishes, refusing Annabel's and Marty's help, telling them I need the company "down in the pit." Ours is one of the few houses still standing with a sunken living room, all the rage in 1970s Arizona. Everyone else in the neighborhood has spent their $20,000 on a cement truck and the appropriate cubic footage of concrete to fill in their conversation pits. Forgive the symbolism, but it happens to be where we have had some of our deepest conversations. And most difficult. This is where I have collected clues to why misery has so much say in our lives.

While John clanks dishes in the kitchen, and Annabel and Marty talk about all the places they will take Daisy tomorrow, one of those conversations replays in my head.

"Tell me John. Tell me what eats away at you."

"I don't know, Charlotte."

"How can you not know?"

"It's not as simple as everyone makes it out to be. I can't just materialize some problem that can be fixed. I know that would make everyone happy. But it's not that easy."

"I'm not saying it's easy. I just want to know what the source of your pain is."

"The source of my pain is life."

"But your life isn't painful."

"Not like yours. Is that what you mean? I must be a weak person if I can't withstand the small inconveniences of life. And meanwhile there are people with great hardship skipping through their day."

"No, I didn't say that. I'm certainly not skipping."

John dropped his chin to his chest, closed his eyes and exhaled forcefully. "I'm sorry," he said. "I know you aren't skipping. That was a callous choice of words on my part. I am sorry."

"It's OK. "

"I'm sorry."

"It's alright."

"I feel like I'm being eaten alive."

"I know. By something in your past. Right? By some regret. Is that what it is?"

John looked into space at a far-off memory. Then his gaze suddenly broke. "So what are you doing with your time these days,

Charlotte, working on an online degree in psychology?"

"Sarcasm. That usually means you're coming out of it. Or going back in."

"You're going to get an A in that class, that's for sure."

"I just want to help you, John."

"Nobody can help me, Charlotte. I'm sure you've done enough research on this condition to know you can't fix me."

"Fix you, no. Help you, yes."

"You can't Charlotte. Nobody can. There is nothing that can change this."

"How are you so sure? Don't you want to change it?"

"Nothing can, Charlotte."

"So, we're destined to live like this forever?"

"No. You're not."

"I'm not?"

"No. You're not the one with the problem. You don't have to live with it."

"Since when did we become *me* and *you* and not *us*? It is *our* problem, John. I'm not going anywhere."

"You didn't know what you were getting into, Charlotte. It's not fair to you."

"Are you going to leave me because I can't see?"

"I would never leave you."

"Did you know exactly what you were getting in to?"

"I think so. Yes."

"Would you leave me if I sustained a brain injury in a car accident? That would not be something you could have predicted before walking down the aisle."

"I would never leave you, Charlotte. I made a promise. To you and to God. I wouldn't break it."

"Then, why would you think I would?"

"I don't know. I just don't want you to live in misery."

I wish I could say it isn't misery. But a lot of the time, it is.

"There is nothing that would make me wish away my life with you, John. The joy we have is pure joy."

"And the sorrow is pure sorrow. That's my contribution to the marriage."

"You don't bring me sorrow, John. This thing we're battling together. That brings sorrow. But there is no such thing as a life without that. I learned that a long time ago."

"Why does it have to be that way?"

"I don't know. I guess because this is not heaven."

"Falling in love with you was heaven."

"Falling in love is heaven." I picked up his hand and squeezed it. "And now we're back to earth and we have to make all of this work."

"Why couldn't heaven have lasted?"

"Oh, now I see," I said. "You thought I was the cure."

"No."

"Yes, you did."

"No. I guess maybe I hoped love was the cure."

"That's a heavy burden to place on our marriage, John. You can't do that."

"No, it's not like that, Charlotte. My mother used to tell us 'love is the answer to every question.'"

"Well, it clearly is not the answer to this one. We have loved as much and as intensely as two people can and it has provided no answers." I didn't like that I was going to such a defeatist's place, and I knew it wasn't good for John, but I couldn't turn myself around. "I just don't see how it's possible for you to be so miserable around someone you are supposed to love."

"Well, I guess we're even, Charlotte. It looks like we are both surprised to learn that our being together didn't fix me. Oh, Charlotte, if you knew—" He stopped and took a heavy breath.

"If I knew what, John? I'm trying to know. Please help me to know."

"If you knew what it felt like to be depressed, you wouldn't take this personally."

"I know what it feels like. I also know neither one of us were depressed for the first six months of knowing each other. Just being in each other's presence was pure joy. Where did that go, John? Why can't we have that back again? What was all that?"

"I don't know. Do you find it disturbing that it did not last? Are you surprised it was so short lived."

"I just never could have pictured it ever going away."

John was the first man to love me. I didn't think anyone ever would. I couldn't imagine wanting to sign up for a lifetime of duty to a blind woman. I do have moments of deep depression myself and those didn't just start when I married John. I have to admit, I never considered that when he asked me to marry him. I guess my self-centeredness, my need to love and be loved, blinded me. John thought about how his suffering would spill over into mine. I never thought how it would spill the other way. Not until it was apparent I would be completely without sight. And then I only thought of how my disability would inconvenience him. I didn't think about how my suffering might cause his. But what could we have done after already falling in love? You can't undo that. Sooner or later, there will be separation. I guess we opted for later, for holding on to what we have until we can't hold on to it anymore. And as much as we live in desperation, we haven't reached the point yet where we have lost our grasp. I just hope we are still holding on after I have said what I need to say.

4

Cinnamon Sadness

I awake in the middle of the night gasping for air, hearing my voice claiming that I can't breath, theorizing one of my lungs has been stolen.

"I don't want to die. I don't want to."

I am crying without tears as I often do in my dreams.

John jumps from his sleep and put his arms around me. "It's OK, Honey. It's OK. You're OK. You're not dying."

I am angry that John does not know what is going on, and he won't take my word for it.

"It's not OK, John. It's not. I am dying."

"No, you're not, Charlotte. It's OK. Calm down now and lay here with me." He pulls me down with him, his arms still wrapping me tight. A warm calm envelops me as my chest meets his. It has been a long time since our hearts have touched. I feel protected and sheltered, the way I did back then, the moment of our first embrace. How long can we make this last? I am desperate to make it stay, but I know it won't. I have more information now than I had then. Far more. If I am going to be honest, I will have to admit something highly disturbing about myself. I wanted John to take care of me. I didn't get married for that reason. I know I didn't. I got married to be with John. I would not have let another man take care of me. It had to be John. It felt romantic to me—my arms wrapped around his neck as he carried me across Longfellow Creek. His hand on my arm as we crossed the street. My hand in his as we walked through the grocery store. When we married, there wasn't a doubt in my mind, or in his, that John was going to take care of me. It never crossed my mind that I would be taking care of him.

I wouldn't mind at all if I knew how. I envy John for the things he has to do for me. They may be demanding, but they are not complicated. There is no mystery involved in fulfilling my needs. If we are walking, you hold my arm. If we are cooking, you carve the roast. If we are checking the mail, you read the return addresses to me. If we are shopping, you check the tags for the right size. But what do you do for someone who wakes up hating life?

I can't say I enjoy the reversal of roles, even as much as I have always hated the feeling of being a burden to someone. I am coming to the surprising and dismaying revelation that I would rather be a burden than take on a burden. What kind of a spouse am I? What kind of lover thinks that way? We carry such different burdens. No one could argue that my blindness is in any way my fault. But no matter how hard I try to convince myself that depression is a disease, I still find myself blaming John for not just deciding to get over it. He could fix himself if he wanted to. This is the belief I hold at my core, and it is the one that is the most destructive. But I can't help harboring it, even though, if you were to ask me straight out, I would tell you it's not his fault.

But I have learned all kinds of survival skills. There is a sign that depression is about to set in. It is the smell of cinnamon. Whenever John's feeling down, he eats red hots. It took me awhile to make the connection because he usually does this sometime in the middle of the night when he can't sleep. He watches infomercials and eats red hots. I'm grateful for the sign because it allows me to prepare. By prepare, I do not mean like what you might do when a storm is blowing in. Board up the windows, bring in the lawn chairs, clear the rain gutters, fill the bathtub with water and close all interior doors. No, I mean prepare as in build walls. I construct a fortress. I know the person who is supposed to be my best friend will be unavailable for awhile. I've come to pretend he's on vacation, a camping trip or someplace where I can't reach him. Meanwhile, I stay inside my fortress.

 හ%ෲ%හ%ෲ%හ%ෲ%හ%ෲ%හ%ෲ

Given the cinnamon on John's breath this morning, it probably wasn't a good idea for me to suggest we go to Mass with Marty, Annabel and Daisy. We haven't gone in I don't know how many months. Of course, we have to have an argument before we can get there. Fortunately, we don't argue in front of our guests. We argue about our guests. We argue in our bedroom with our door closed. I want to know why he has been so aloof and absent while his family is here. He jumps at the chance to run any errand he can. And I am even tempted to think he purposely forgets stuff at the store so he can go back again and get it. Of course, I would never openly accuse him of that. Anyway, he tells me we should just go to Mass without him because he has a headache.

"I can't make any more excuses for you, John. They will think you don't want them here."

"It's not an excuse, Charlotte. You know, other people besides you can have things wrong with them. No one accuses you of making up your physical frailties."

"I never accused you, John. I just said it's going to look

like you are making excuses not to be with them, so if you can find a way to push through the pain—"

"No, I can't push through. I'm a whimp. I'm not the strong person you are."

"I can't believe you would use that kind of sarcasm with me."

"Yes, people in your condition should be allowed to bully anyone they want."

"I'm not bullying you, John. That's not my style." Even if it was, I'm too busy walking on eggs to accomplish any bullying.

"OK, let's just get through this day," he says. "This morning."

"It won't be all that bad, getting back to church."

"No, I guess not."

"I know it's not the way or the time we would have chosen to go back. We need to go to Confession, but we can just abstain from Communion until we get there."

"Oh, *we* need confession, huh? You have examined my conscience and come to that conclusion."

"No, I haven't. But I do know, from living in the same house with you, that you have missed quite a number of Sunday Masses, which requires you to go to Confession, if you remember your Catechism."

"Now who's being sarcastic? Anyway, we had a reason for missing Mass. We have both been sick."

"Sick?"

"Well, you know. You with your eyes and me with my depression."

"You know that's not our reason, John. We are able to get out to the grocery store."

"I'm just so exhausted by the end of the week. I have demands on me all week long. I just need a day to stay home and rest."

"You are exhausted from taking care of me. I'm very sorry to be such a burden."

I didn't say it like I was sorry, but I really am. I don't think it was a good idea for someone with John's condition to be saddled with mine. But here we are.

"I didn't say that, Charlotte. Why do you insist on making me into such a bad person?"

"I thought that's the game we were playing. Who can make the other person feel crummiest about themselves. The winner gets to go guilt free, proving nothing is ever their fault."

We stand together at Mass, trying to appear as if we are what we should be—happy to have found each other, happy to be together in the presence of all the angels, watching salvation unfold. But instead, we are both stewing the words we had spewed earlier. Spew and stew is the cycle we have fallen into. It is disturbing because it wasn't that long ago that we had bliss.

The priest reads the gospel: *...Blessed are the poor in spirit: for theirs is the kingdom of heaven ... Blessed are they who mourn: for they shall be comforted...*

Daisy steps in between me and John and is holding our hands. Then, in what would seem like a randomly spontaneous move, she pulls our two hands in front of her and places them together, squeezing them from the outside to make sure they stick, and the next thing I know, John's hand is clasped around mine. I feel tears sting my eyes as I realize this is the way we started—holding hands at Mass. We have fallen so far, but Daisy proves—in a single movement of two hands being forced to share the same parcel of air—that we can start the ascent from anywhere on the slope.

৩৩)❄(৪৩)❄(৩৩)❄(৪৩)❄(৩৩)❄(৪৩)❄(৩৩)❄(৪৩)

If you want to make sure your out of town guests get to do something they can't do back home, you can pretty much bet the Ostrich Festival will fit the bill. Daisy laughs so hard when she sees grown men and women riding those large gangly birds around the race track.

John would have probably made some excuse to get out of going if it wasn't for the fact that we went straight to the festival after Mass.

Annabel, John and I are lying on a grassy hill overlooking the festival as Marty takes Daisy on the carnival rides.

"Remember when you were a kid, lying down on the grass and looking up into the sky?" Annabel asks.

"Yeah," John nods. "I remember."

"I haven't looked up into the sky in I don't know how long," Annabel says.

"I guess adults forget to do stuff like that," John says.

"Remember how happy it made you?"

"Yeah."

"Like being one with the universe or something."

"Yeah. Like that."

"Like being free. Like nothing is pressing down on you. No ceilings. Just vast openness. An invitation."

I am not in this conversation because I have nothing to add, but I am enjoying the imagery.

"That cloud looks like a baby harp seal," Annabel says.

"Yeah it does."

"Or a guinea pig."

"I've got to go find a rest room." John stands, brushes off his khaki shorts and clomps down the hill.

"Sure is beautiful weather," Annabel says after some moments of silence. "I could get used to this."

"You and Marty should think about moving down. I have

to say I don't miss the grey at all."

"Would be nice. Can't say that shoveling snow is among my favorite pass times."

I smile and have a renewed appreciation for the sun on my face. I think of a picture I once saw of Lily, squinting into the sun, the light glinting off her apple cheeks.

"What do you think it was like for Lily to be depressed?" I ask.

"I don't know," Annabel says. "I don't think her depression was too severe. They say it had to do with chemical changes in her body as she got older."

"But she did suffer her share of losses,"

"Yes. Losing Frank was the big one."

"She took Pablo's passing pretty hard too. And Bev, of course."

"Yeah, but she rebounded after those."

"Yep. But Frank. That was a different matter altogether."

They used to find her sleeping on his grave," Annabel says. "She would pack a lunch and take the bus and camp out at the cemetery. She'd have her ear buds in and be listening to their favorite songs and she'd sit there and draw until she fell asleep."

"What would she draw?"

"What she always drew. All kinds of wild animals. Oh yes, and she would bring him a stick each time she came. She was always mystified to see that it was never there when she returned. The silk flowers, the flags, the toys—all those things people bring to graves—they would stay. All faded and weather-worn. But the sticks would disappear. Everyone else knew the maintenance man saw those sticks as something that didn't belong there and cleaned them up. Lily thought Frank somehow collected them and took them with him to heaven when no one was looking."

"I wonder if it's true what everyone says, that a person

can't make another person happy. A person can surely make another person miserable, right? So I will ask again, how is it that my love is not enough?"

John comes up the hill and settles back into his spot next to me. "So, what are we talking about?"

"Lily's losses," Annabel says.

"And that's all?"

"Well, we were also talking a bit about yours," she admits.

"My losses?"

"Well, whatever it is that makes you sad sometimes. What is the root of it, John? You've never told me."

"The root of it? I don't know. But I remember when I first felt it."

Something about Annabel makes John talk about things he never would with me. I am jealous and grateful. More grateful, I guess. I am desperate for information, and at this point, I don't care by what method it comes.

"It was the day I didn't make the football team," John says into space, "and it lasted for a good six weeks."

"Did you ever try out again?" I ask.

"No, I never did. I probably should have, but I was so scarred by not making it the first time, I didn't want to take the chance of sinking into another depression."

"Makes sense," Annabel says.

"Yeah. But I remember that day I came home so despondent. I had thought I was going to make it since I was not a small kid. And I had gotten lots of practice in backyard football. There were always foster kids to play with. And Lily. She was a pretty good offensive lineman."

"Really?" I say. "She played with you guys?"

"Oh, yeah. And on the day I came home crushed, she sat on the couch with me and watched *Rudy*. I should have learned something from that movie and tried out again the next year."

"Yeah, but you may have been right not to risk it," Annabel says. "It's not worth weeks of depression."

"Yeah, but it wasn't really the failure that depressed me. It was my guilt."

"About what?" I ask.

"About how nice Lily treated me that day. I didn't deserve it."

"What do you mean?" I say. "Why wouldn't you deserve to be comforted?"

"I deserved to be knocked down a few notches. But Lily never gave anyone what they deserved."

"I don't understand, John," I say. "What do you mean by deserving to be knocked down?"

"Now, don't go getting psycho-analytical on me. I don't know what I meant. I'm just talking."

"I don't know, John," Annabel says. "You're not one to just talk. You're too deep a thinker for that."

"Really? You want to hear one of my deep thoughts?"

"Sure."

"Oh, never mind," he says waving his hand.

"No," I say, "go ahead."

"No, we better wrap it up here. We've all gotten enough sun."

Exhausted from the day's fun, Daisy crashes as soon as we get home and have a bite to eat. Annabel and Marty turn in right after. John collapses in the bed and clicks on the TV, channel surfing between nature documentaries and crime shows. I slip under the covers next to him and point my face at the screen, as if I can watch it. I decide this could be a good time to tell him the secret I've been keeping. If it doesn't go well, Annabel might be able to help us pick up the pieces. But I can't seem to find the words. Not even inside my head. So, I turn to a different topic.

"What was it, John?" I ask, resting my head on his chest. "What was it you were going to say?"

"Hmmm?"

"Back at the festival? What were you going to say about your deep thought?"

"My deep thought?"

"About Lily."

"Oh," John says. "You want to hear my deep thought about Lily. Well, it just occurred to me the other day. I know your aunt's love saved you, Charlotte, but Lily's love makes no difference to me."

"Makes no difference?

"Yes. None. I know she loved me profoundly, and it makes no difference."

"How could it not make a difference?"

"It was based on something false."

"What do you mean?"

"She didn't really know who I am. Lily was simple. She only saw the good in people. There was a lot more of me than she ever saw. And it wasn't good."

"You are good, John. We all make mistakes in our youth. And we all have our life-long faults. But you are undeniably good."

"No use arguing with you about this. You are clearly biased."

"I admit that I am. Just a bit. But I'm still right about one thing. You deserved every bit of Lily's love. Because I know that you loved her."

"With all my heart. Since the very beginning. But it was easy. My earliest memories are of her. She worked at a grocery store, and every week when she got paid, she'd bring me a stuffed animal—at least in the seasons when grocery stores carry stuffed animals. I ended up with lots of chickens, bunnies and reindeer. My favorite was this little fox that came with a heart in its mouth, which I asked my mom to cut off the day after Valentine's Day. I called her Penny. Lily told me I should call her 7.99 because that's how much she cost. She would tell me that every time we played with her, and then she would laugh and laugh. We used to get every stuffed animal in the house and pile them on top of ourselves on the bed, and from inside that dark, stuffy heap, those animals would embark on all kind of amazing adventures. I don't know why they had to be piled on top of us for that to work, but that's just the precedent somebody set. And then even when I got older, Lily was my touchstone. It just seemed like everything was right when she was around. Not always predictable. But right. I never found it possible to be depressed when she was around. I mean, everything was so unexpected, it was like having your brain rewired and having the rewiring take you so off guard that all your energy, including all your negative energy, was sucked up by trying to understand the novelty of what was happening. Everything she did was so original, like at every moment, something was being reinvented in the cosmos—and whatever it is that locks us all into familiar and predictable brain patterns was just suspended. You know what I mean?"

"No, not really."

"Let me give you an example, then."

He tells me he could give many, but he decides on this one:

It was a very windy day, and Lily and I had just gotten out of the car in the Church parking lot. She started frantically pointing at the top of the flag pole.

"John, look! Look!"

"What?"

The American flag had the tallest pole and flew just above the two others—Vatican and Washington. The three poles were close enough together that the wind was able to blow the American flag in such a way that it had gotten stuck on the top of the Vatican flag pole.

This is the kind of thing Lily would have typically laughed at. But not when it had to do with Old Glory. She had just watched a documentary on the history of the flag and how it had been disrespected by different groups throughout history. The show included a segment on the care and protocol connected with flying the Star Spangled Banner.

"John, we have to fix it," Lily insisted.

"Don't worry, Lily, the wind will take care of it. It will blow off of there."

"No, it might take too long. We have to fix it now."

"How would we do that?"

"Go up the pole."

"I can't do that."

"I seen people do it."

"Like who?"

"Firemen. They cute too."

"No, firefighters slide *down* poles, Lily."

"They can go up if they wan-. They firemen."

"Well, I'm not a fireman."

"We can get a ladder."

"Lily, that flag is a long way up there. We better let the wind take care of it."

"You don't care about the flag."

"I do, Lily, but there's nothing we can do about it. And there's no harm leaving it there."

"It look silly. I don' like the flag look silly."

"Why?"

"It make me feel bad. I know what it feel like. I got my skirt stuck in my underwear. Gwenny laugh at me. I was dancing and she was laughing. And then the guy I dancing with laugh at me."

And that's how you learn to think in all new ways when you know someone like Lily.

5

The Deep Well

I cry in lieu of sleep, wrapped in John's arms. I don't want him to know how worried I am, but really, it all poured out. He just lies quietly, stroking my hair, kissing the top of my head. I don't know why I am such a mess about this, and I hope my mess doesn't send John into the darkness. I really have over-reacted to this considering I don't know Jimmy and Georgia that well. There have been a number of national news stories that hit me like this. A particular school shooting. The bombing of a particular federal building, containing a day care center. A particular earthquake in which they found a mother and child curled up together under the rubble. I could weep for hours. And then other tragedies, some with even greater numbers of casualties, have no effect on me at all. Maybe it has to do with shattered joy. Daisy had just come into their lives. Annabel and Marty were going to take her to meet her new grandparents in Minneapolis after making a stop off here in Phoenix. Jimmy and Georgia were to return home from Mexico tomorrow following a ten-day vacation in Veracruz.

My guess is they got a little too adventurous and strayed

from the tourist areas. Annabel said they've never been to Mexico before.

Annabel and Marty flew out last night, as soon as they heard Jimmy and Georgia had been arrested for drug possession. Officials rounded up a number of "suspects" at a bus station in Boca del Rio. It would be frightening enough to be arrested for drugs in the U.S. But in Mexico, it's terrifying. Daisy will be staying with us until Annabel and Marty can, please God, help get Jimmy and Georgia released.

I'm happy to have her, happy there is something we can do to help, but I feel a loss at Annabel's leaving. Her presence here was going to help us somehow. I was going to get clues or insights and maybe even courage to tell John what I need to tell him. Annabel understands John in a way that I don't. I know I am supposed to say that it feels like I've been with him forever, and nobody could possibly know him like I do. But it really just seems like a short while that I have known him.

The day we met, I had just come home from the hospital after my eye surgery. The doctors had told me I would spend the rest of my life seeing less and less, until finally one day, probably in the not-too-distant future, I would see nothing at all. Well, they didn't phrase it quite that way, but that's what I gleaned from the prognosis.

John's voice was the kindest I'd ever heard. I really didn't want to entertain visitors that day, of course. Just Jesus. But Jesus in the Blessed Sacrament is always accompanied by another person, so it was worth it to wash my face, braid my hair and make myself ready to face another human being. If I was to follow in my aunt's footsteps, which is what I always promised myself I would do, I could never consider myself too old for braids. Also as tribute to Aunt Winnie, in the interest of seeing life as a gift no matter how hard things get, I looked for the most colorful thing I could find in my closet. So I put on a sun dress with hot pink and bright yellow flowers and wore a white scarf around my shoulders. A bit bolder than my personality, but I had, after all, been to Paris and Venice and Madrid, I reminded myself. People who have travelled and seen art galleries can pull this kind of thing off. People like that don't have to wear black and khaki and navy blue as I have worn most of my life. Navy blue begs people not to notice you. I've been begging all my life. It was a habit formed as a kid. I just wanted to disappear. Especially when ugly words started flying, and even in the moments when they weren't, since I always knew they could, at any minute.

John started coming regularly to bring me Communion and homemade tomato soup and take my trash out, throw loads of laundry in and pull the weeds. I had no family in town, so his was the only help I had. I grew to crave his smile. The day after he'd been over, that smile would be pressed in my mind. I kept seeing it, like a tattoo on my memory. I would see it all day long, like those images that form before your vision after you look at a bright light. But the effects of the light were not enough. I wanted to see the light itself. I would think, "I've got to figure out a way to see his smile again." I actually fell in love with it. First the smile and then John.

I have to admit, I did not fall in love with a man who suffered from depression. I found that out later. I have to give John credit. He knew exactly what he was falling in love with, and he fell anyway. That's what kind of man he is. Me, I didn't know, and I ask myself now if I would have still fallen.

Early on, I thought my love was going to save him. I thought being with someone you're crazy about would benefit your sanity. I guess I had a lot to learn about love. And Sanity.

I can't say John didn't warn me.

"You are the type of girl I would want to marry, Charlotte. If I could."

"Why can't you?"

"I am not the type that should be married, Charlotte. I would be no good for a wife."

"How can you say that? You're one of the most incredible men I've ever met."

"You've only seen the best side of me."

"And you've only seen the best side of me."

"I'm not talking about just putting on your best face for someone. I'm talking about something far more serious."

"Like what?"

He grabbed his tablet and pulled up a message board titled "living with someone who lives with depression."

One woman said she'd aged twenty years in the one she'd spent with her spouse. Other women complained that they are so worn down, nothing is enjoyable anymore. Arguments arise out of and about nothing. They are accused of trying to make their spouses angry and asking stupid questions. There are shouting matches followed by silent treatments. Those can last days. Until the woman ends up apologizing because the man makes her feel like she is the one in the wrong. She spends most nights crying herself to sleep, alone. She tries to be counselor, but her "client" is rarely ever grateful. She is taken for granted. She tries to keep her partner's suicidal thoughts at bay, recommends therapists, encourages the taking of medication. She lives with unpredictable outcomes and copious criticism. She is always blamed. She is told to shut up or silenced with the F-word. She feels worthless. She loves her husband but hates the way moods take control of their lives.

I came to the conclusion that if I were to marry someone like this, I would spend the rest of my life feeling the way my mama made me feel. I can't say if she suffered from depression or just mean and ornery rottenness. I had never thought about the possibility of a mental illness. Now the man I was in love with was telling me, if I stayed with him long enough, he would end up treating me like I was treated the whole time I was growing up. I found it difficult to believe on a number of levels. First, why was lightening striking me twice? Why would I have to deal with that throughout my childhood and then face it again as an adult, in a whole new scenario, with a whole new person? Second, I could not picture John ever uttering an unkind word to anyone. He was the kindest, most loving and lovable man I had ever known. The men who brought so much sadness to the women who loved them could not be anything like the man I knew.

I began to adopt the theory that John was finding a nice, gentle way of breaking it off. As wonderful and kind as he was, who could blame him? Who could wonder why someone would not choose to be saddled with the responsibilities of caring for a disabled spouse?

But John insisted he had another side, and he insisted I read further about the misery of living with it.

I did my research, but it didn't much matter. I refused to believe it could ever apply to us. Surely, our love would be enough to keep us out of the ditch.

I was wrong.

The scariest conversation we ever had came just before our second anniversary. I knew it was a mistake to try to have a conversation like this while John was deep in the pit. Conversations in the pit should be restricted to the weather or football scores or what kind of lunch meat we will buy that week. And even those should be kept to a minimum because they carry with them the risk of sounding like accusations. They are never intended that way, but something as simple as "how much time left in the game?" can be understood as "Would you please, for the love of Pete, turn that stinkin' game off already! All you ever do is watch sports!"

And the question of "Should we try the turkey instead of the roast beef this time?" will be interpreted as, "Your diet is atrocious and you really need to start eating leaner because just look at those fat rolls, hanging over your belt."

But for some reason, despite all my internal warnings and the instinctual prudence that had been so highly useful in stopping me from treading too heavily on cracked egg shells, I launched us into a perilous place with a single observation.

"Can you believe it's been almost two years? Seems like yesterday and yet, it seems like a lifetime too. Like I can't really even remember a time without you."

"You didn't know what you were getting into, Charlotte. You wouldn't have chosen this. And I am sorry."

I didn't know what to say. It was a difficult statement to argue with if I was going to be honest.

"You would not make the same decision all over again. But you can't say I didn't warn you, Charlotte. Remember? I did try to talk sense into you. But you still insisted you wanted to be with me."

"I'm not one to question past decisions, John. We go forward from here."

"I guess I got my answer."

"No, John."

"I told you it gets ugly. But if you feel like you got a raw deal, there's nothing holding you here."

"Nothing holding me? How can you say that? Love is holding me."

I imagined he was staring at his hands, his palms resting formally on his thighs.

"You don't feel love holding you?" I asked.

There was a pause, like some calculations were being made. "Right now, I don't feel anything."

"You want me to leave?"

"No."

"No?"

"I want you to stay. But if you have to leave, I understand."

"I don't know how to live with someone who doesn't love me. But I guess I can learn how to do it."

"I didn't say I don't love you."

"You said you don't feel anything."

"I don't. But I love you."

"I don't understand what that means."

"I don't feel anything. I don't know if I ever will."

"So how can you say you love me?"

"Because I know that I do."

"I don't understand the not feeling anything. I love you so much it hurts."

"I don't understand it either. But this is what it is. I wish it wasn't. Believe me, I wish it could be different. But there's no guarantee I'm ever getting out of this again. This may be all there is the rest of our lives. Can you live with that?"

"It sounds like you are trying to get rid of me."

He didn't respond, but I think he was shaking his head.

"Are you?"

"I'm trying to tell you it's OK if you can't be here. I'm trying to tell you I don't have the energy or even the desire to run my side of this thing and I don't know if I ever will."

"This thing? It's a marriage, John. This thing is love. Doesn't that mean anything to you? You're just going to give up on it?"

"I can't do any better than this, Charlotte. It isn't fair to either one of us to pretend. So I'm not going to."

"OK. If it makes no difference to you, I won't stay."

"OK."

"If it makes no difference to you."

"No. I can't really say that anything makes a difference anymore."

"OK. I don't understand that, John. But OK."

"I know you deserve better than this. You deserve a life."

"I thought that's what we were trying to build here."

"I can't build anything, Charlotte. It's all I can do to keep from tearing things down."

"Why?"

"Why? I don't know. It just is."

And to that, I could say no more.

I didn't leave. I just waited. Life went on, painfully, but as expected, eventually returning to normal in all its appearances, and we never had a discussion that intense again. We had learned something. We had both taken the conversation to a place we never wanted to see again. Since then, we have always stopped short. Our discussions can be difficult, but not devastating. They are typically followed by days of silence. John just doesn't speak. These are the hardest times. I can't read faces any more. I rely on my ears for everything. Without words, I am at the bottom of a well. I really don't want to go there right now, and I hope he doesn't make me after hearing what I have to say.

6

Secrets

I have a dream that Lily is pushing me in a wheelchair down a long, narrow corridor. We are moving closer and closer toward the door at the end of the hall. I know that when the door opens, we will be two or three stories up, and there will be no stairs or ramps. I know this because I have seen this place from the outside and have noticed that the door was in that very strange place, and I feared that some child would open it and fall out. Lily is pushing me faster and faster toward the end of the hallway, and my stomach is doing flips at the thought of bursting through the door and plummeting to my death. But as the door opens, there is indeed ground beneath my wheels—very bumpy ground, covered with a thick carpet of pine needles that crack and pop as the wheelchair passes over them. We are in a lush forest, as endless as it is green, like the ones Tolkien liked to create. Lily begins to laugh and pushes me faster and soon we come to a clearing. A man with Down syndrome sits cross-legged before a pile of sticks. I think for a second maybe his is going to start a fire, but then I realize, these sticks are not kindling. They are each too unique and I feel he understands they should be treasured, not burned, because of their uniqueness. He smiles at me and motions for me to sit down.

I am awakened by John's shaving cream can falling onto the tile floor and rolling, and John's swear word under his breath.

"She never comes to me in my dreams," he says out loud. "Or any other time."

"Who?"

"Lily."

I lay in silence trying to figure out how he knew the contents of my dream.

"Everyone else in the family has heard from her. Some hear from her regularly. I haven't heard anything. I haven't even had a dream about her. Don't you find that odd?"

"I don't know. But it bothers you, huh?"

"Yeah, I guess it does. I would like to see her again. Even if it were just a dream. I could see her for a few minutes, at least. You never even met her and she is in your dreams."

"How do you know that?"

"You said her name in your sleep."

"I think Lily and I have a special connection because if it hadn't been for her, I never would have met you."

It was Lily's desire to bring her husband Communion when he was sick that inspired her to take the ministry of care training. Because of her disability and the fact that she couldn't drive, someone had to partner with her, so John went through the training with her and accompanied her in visiting the sick. After Lily died, John carried on without her. And that is why, some years later, after one of my eye surgeries, John brought Communion to my home.

He comes to my bedside now and kisses me. He is in his uniform. It's still dark out. All the city park rangers are convening at the lake for a quarterly meeting.

"Are you going to be alright for a few hours?" he asks. "I'll try to get off early if I can."

"We'll be fine. But I better get up and be ready for her. She'll no doubt be up before the sun again."

I was a little off. Daisy gave the sun a five-minute head start. She walked straight to the window, just like yesterday morning.

"Your mommy and daddy are still in Mexico, Daisy," I tell her. "They'll be back soon, though. What would you like for breakfast?"

Daisy and I make quite a pair, the two of us. She needs to communicate without words, and I need to understand without sight. John has stocked the cabinet with a large number of sugar cereals. It's what you do if you have a kid visiting you. You stock up on every food item the parents would never give them. It is a bit difficult to determine from her pointing whether she wants the Chocochoochoos or the Apple Snaps. Or the Raisin Crunchers or DinoCrisps. I get them all down for her. All seven boxes of cereal. She chooses the Frosted Bananarambas, most likely because there's a picture of a very famous monkey on the front.

"Oh yeah, that's a good one," I tell her.

She is quiet for a while, studying the pictures, I think, while I go get the bowl, spoon and milk. Then I hear the paper rustling and some crunching and realize she has reached her hand down in and come up with a fistful of artificially flavored, artificially colored, sugar-laden breakfast. John must have opened the box and had some this morning.

"Let's put it in a bowl with some milk, Daisy," I say.

"No," she says, crunching.

"OK, should I pour the milk in a glass for you to drink?"

I hear no response, so I get a glass. I don't want to dip my finger into someone else's drink, aside from John's, to see if the glass if full. So I decide to rely only on my hearing. Not a drop spilled – neither by me or Daisy. The cereal is not so neatly consumed, and I tell myself I should clean it up before someone steps on it and makes cereal dust. I get down on the ground and feel for it. But Daisy has left the kitchen, so I have to follow her. I realize I have only my sense of hearing to find out what she is doing. Mothers who see can be washing dishes while watching their babies play across the room. Blind mothers must remain close to their children, I suppose. But where else should they want to be?

"Daisy?"

She doesn't answer, but I can hear her breathing. Her breaths are loud and often have a grunting tone to them. I figure it must be tonsils and adenoids. Annabel did mention she was scheduled for surgery soon. I see her form moving in front of the window.

"Daisy, are you waiting for your mommy and daddy to come home?" I take her by the hand, lead her to the easy chair and lift her onto my lap. "When I was a little girl, I did a lot of waiting too."

I used to stand by the window and wait for my aunt to come back, the morning after she left. After a few days, I'd quit waiting. Then, when I least expected it, she'd flurry through the door with some large amount of color trailing after her in the form of a scarf or a bouquet of balloons. How I loved all the color she brought into my life. And she'd ask me, "Can you keep a secret, Charlotte?" And I'd always swear that I could, and she would tell me some important news, and I'd always wonder why she wanted it kept secret. One time the secret was that she was going to Europe. Another time, it was that she was taking piano lessons. Another time, she told me she was getting a parrot. I never saw evidence that any of these things came to pass, but I always enjoyed the idea that they were going to happen.

"Can you keep a secret, Daisy?"

The little girl turns her gaze from the window and looks close into my eyes, like she knows that this is the only distance at which my eyes could connect with hers. "You won't tell anybody my secret, right? No one else in the entire world knows this."

She nods and returns her eyes to what lies outside the window. I look out that way too, trying to imagine what she is seeing, though I can see nothing but whiteness.

"I'm going to have a baby."

7

Unsafe Pasta

I am proud of myself for being able to get dinner on the table for John. I have spaghetti with Marinara sauce, an iceberg and tomato salad and Italian bread ready for him when he walks through the door. I am feeling quite successful and impressed with my own ingenuity. I had Daisy right by my side as I prepared the food. She was happy to be helping me. Under my direction, she set the table. I don't know that she got everything exactly right because I didn't have time to go to each place setting and feel for the accuracy of where the silverware was placed. But generally, I know there is enough of everything. In honor of Daisy, I have a vase of desert marigolds on the table. We cut them off the bush in the back yard. They are the ones that people say look like yellow daisies and grow so prevalently on small bushes in desert landscapes. I had Daisy grasp them one by one as I held the scissors, and she guided my hand to snip them. I was surprised how smart she is about my blindness. It didn't take her long to figure out what I can and cannot do, and it makes me wonder if maybe she had been with some blind people back at the home in Jamaica.

"Ah, you two have been busy," John says as he sits down at the table.

"Nah, nah," I hear Daisy protesting.

"What? What is it Daisy?" John asks.

Daisy slaps the table. From the sound of it, she is pounding on the spot adjacent to hers.

"She wants you to sit next to her, John."

No matter how sunk he might have been before coming through that door, he is going to have to come up to the surface, at least long enough to get a breath of joy. Even if it's just a single breath.

He moves to his new seat, at her command. "OK, Daisy, I'll sit with you."

He jumps up again. "Gotta get the butter."

"Sorry, I forgot."

"No problem." He sits back down again. "You want butter, Daisy?"

"Oh," I say after putting the first bite into my mouth. "Pasta's a bit overcooked. Sorry about that."

"It's fine. How come you decided to make pasta today?"

"I don't know. I guess because we all had to eat."

"Did you forget it was on the stove?"

"No."

"How'd it get over-cooked?"

"I don't know. I guess it just cooked faster than I thought."

"How'd you drain it?"

"With a colander."

"I mean, wasn't it hard to do with the boiling water and Daisy with you and everything?"

"No, not really. What are you getting at?"

"I just don't know how safe it is—you cooking with a small child around."

"It's safe. Why are you being so silly?"

"I don't think I'm being that silly. The pasta is clearly over-cooked. And not by a small amount. Something went wrong in the kitchen."

"Well, I don't think it's that bad."

"Yummy," Daisy says. "More."

"See? Daisy backs me up on this." I reach for the bowl of spaghetti. I miss the mark slightly and the bowl lifts off the table and returns with a clumsy thud.

"Here," John says. "I'll get her some more."

"Those were the first words she has said to us," I say. "She must really like my crummy spaghetti."

"I didn't say it was crummy."

"Well, thank you Daisy," I say. "I am glad you are enjoying the meal."

"I am enjoying it too," John says. "It's very good."

His polite compliment is too late. I already know what he is thinking. I'm really not surprised. Or at least I shouldn't be.

There is, I guess, some comfort in knowing what you are dealing with. And yet, in some ways, I wish I didn't know so much. Sometimes I get annoyed when my predictions turn out right. But I don't much enjoy being blind-sided either.

When I was a kid, I hated roller coasters. I was petrified of them. I would have never elected to go on one. Ever. But there I was, in the dark one day, all secured into a seat on a ride called Space Mountain. John and I had decided to go to Disneyland for our one-year wedding anniversary. He was sitting beside me, squeezing my hand tight, telling me how much I was going to love the ride.

"Whew," John said, when the ride came to an end. "That's one of my favorite roller coasters."

"What? A roller coaster? Is that what that was?"

"Yeah, you didn't know?"

"It was just all dark in there. I felt like I was being sucked from my seat one minute and crammed back into it the next. You know I would have never agreed to a roller coaster if I had known it was a roller coaster."

"Yeah, so now you've done a roller coaster. And it wasn't so bad, right?"

"I wish you had told me Space Mountain is a roller coaster."

"I didn't really even think about it. I just love the ride."

"I will never go on another one," I said.

It wasn't long after that trip that I realized marriage is like Space Mountain. You know nothing about the ride before you get on, except that so many other people have gone already and many are waiting in line, and it is supposed to be fun. If someone had told me it was a roller coaster, I most certainly would not have gotten on. And yet, I don't regret the ride. But I would never do it again. It's a good thing I didn't know then what I know now, I suppose. I had no idea when I pledged my life to the most wonderful man I had ever met that I would find myself on a roller coaster in the dark.

8

Shock in the Park

There are a couple of kids at the park today who decide Daisy is just too different to deserve a ride on the slide.

"That girl who can't talk. Her can't play here." That's what the little one, maybe about six years old, tells me in a firm, authoritative tone as I sit on the park bench listening to Daisy play. I know right where Daisy is because I can hear her breathing and grunting as she plays. Well, it's not exactly a grunt. It's more of an uncomfortable-sounding exhalation of the air that gets penned up behind her adenoids. John has taken Little Sniff to do his business in the grass. He is taking leave from work to take care of Daisy. I wish he could see I could handle it on my own. It is times like these when I despise my eyes.

The larger girl, about nine years old, stands behind the little one with her hand propped on her hip and her feet spread wide apart, like she is in some $90-per-hour photo shoot, her multicolored geometric-shape embossed shirt dripping off one shoulder and a wide belt gripping her around her thick middle, very short shorts made of white denim covering very little of her plump leg and ankle-height fringy boots made of burnt-orange suede completing the "just out for a romp on the playground" ensemble. I know this because John will be describing everything to me in minute detail, so appalled is he by what transpires.

"Can you tell her to get off?" the little one persists. "Why her can't talk right?"

"She has a special challenge," I say.

"Oh," she flings her hair behind her shoulder. "Tell her to get off the playground."

John returns with Little Sniff, who runs up and snuffles the younger girl on the toe, causing her to step back and flinch, drawing her hands up and turning her shoulder to protect herself from Little Sniff's wet nose, which is slowly and methodically working its way up her shin.

Daisy swings happily next to the forbidden slide.

"I'm sorry," John says "Do you not like doggies?"

The girl just stares at Little Sniff.

"Some dogs she likes," her elder sister speaks for the first time. "But not that one."

The little one looks up into John's face. "Tell that girl she can't play here."

John looks confused. "You mean Daisy?"

"I don't want her to play. Her can't talk right."

"Well, this is a public playground, so you can't decide who plays here."

"But she talks like a monkey," the older one chimes in.

"Where's your mother?" John says, surveying the perimeter of the park.

"At home. I'm baby sitting my little sister."

"Well, you go home and tell your mother she has no business sending you two to the park alone. And as a matter of fact tell her she should not even let you out of the house until you learn some manners. And some grammar. Tell her it could be a very long road she's got in front of her."

"John!" I exclaim. I had never before heard an unkind word slip from his lips, not to child nor adult, not even to rude adult.

The little girls ran off to the playground, keeping to the side where Daisy was not.

"I don't know what's gotten into you."

"I'm sorry, Charlotte," John says. "I've just never seen such rude kids. All the little kids loved Lily. She never had trouble finding anyone to play with."

"They're just kids, Honey. That little one sounds like she has some kind of disability of her own."

"Little kids are not supposed to have those kinds of prejudices. I won't sit back and watch that. I'm sorry, but I won't."

"But there are ways, John, to do it without—"

"I'm not going to stand by and let them say whatever they please about a sweet little girl, Charlotte." He must have given Little Sniff's leash a quick yank because I hear the French bulldog's claws on the concrete skittering toward John as he tries to gain slack around the neck. "I'll wait for you in the car."

If you knew John, you would understand why I am so shocked. Not only has he never lost his cool (in front of me anyway), but he has never been anything but overly attentive. Leaving me there without an escort to the car would be unthinkable to him. He has never left me alone like this.

I call Daisy and make my way to the car. She leads me by the hand. It seems she is watching where my feet step. I am amazed. She gets it.

John is quiet, sitting at the steering wheel.

"Message from Annabel," he says, finally. "The Mexican government won't tell her which jail her mom and dad are in. They were apparently moved from the initial point of incarceration, and authorities either don't know or aren't revealing their location."

At home, I make some ham and cheese sandwiches. John makes himself a salad and eats it while Daisy and I have the lunch I prepared, and then Daisy goes into the family room and switches on the TV.

John disappears into our bedroom, so I join Daisy on the couch. I have never seen the show she landed on, but it sounds like it belongs to that cartoon genre with the ugly artwork and mildly crude humor.

"Do you want to watch a movie, Daisy?"

After many rejected suggestions, I finally get a yes for *Tangled*. I tell her it is about a girl whose very long hair has magical powers. She doesn't seem at all disappointed with her choice. After the movie, we return to the kitchen to make some hot cocoa. John is already in there, eating the sandwich I had made him for lunch.

"Did you like that movie?" John asks her. "Do you want to watch it again?"

The hot cocoa is forgotten and Daisy returns to the couch.

"How come you wanted her to watch it again?" I ask.

"Charlotte, I bought airline tickets for Daisy to go stay with Mom and Dad. Mom will fly out and get her at the end of the week to take her to Seattle."

"What?"

"She will be here Friday morning and leave with Daisy on Saturday."

"When did you decide this? Why didn't you tell me?"

"We just can't take care of her, Charlotte. I had no idea Annabel was going to be gone so long. We've got to get our lives back to normal."

"What do you mean? Our lives have been fine. I've been taking good care of her, haven't I? I've been cooking for her, playing with her. I tell her stories and sing to her."

"Of course, you've been doing a wonderful job, Honey. I just know it's been hard. On both of us."

"No. It hasn't been hard on me, John. Does Annabel want her to go stay with your parents?"

"She was fine with whatever we decided."

"We?"

"Look, Charlotte, I didn't know you'd be upset about it. I thought you'd be relieved."

"No. There is nothing to be relieved about. Daisy has been no problem. At least not for me. And I fail to see how she could be a problem for you since you have pretty much ignored her since the day she came."

"Ignored her? What? I work, Charlotte. I don't have time to sit around and play with Barbies.

"You can't spare a little of yourself for her? You have missed out. And how's it going to be for Daisy? She's going to a whole new place now, with a whole new set of people she's never met."

"Oh, you know my Mom. They'll be fast friends."

"I just don't want her to think we've sent her away because we don't love her."

"Oh yes. We've betrayed her into the hands of a couple of people who will spoil her rotten. If Daisy ends up upset with us for anything, it will be for not sending her there sooner."

I was silent for a good long while.

"Did I ever tell you about what happened when I went on vacation and left my dog Jackal with my parents?" John asks. "I came home, expecting to be greeted with licks and leaps and a furiously wagging tail, and all Jackal could manage was an apathetic look like, 'Oh, it's you. You're back.' It was mystifying and sad and then mom tells me, 'I hope you don't mind I strayed a bit from his Kibbles. We had some filet mignon in the freezer from Christmas that needed to be used up.' Then she tells me how nicely he slept on the foot of her bed and how much he loves his twice daily walks."

I pay his story no response. It is a diversionary tactic and it insults my intelligence. "Why didn't you tell me you were planning this?"

"I just thought it was better this way, and I thought you would agree. Mom and Dad can get to know their newest grandkid this way."

"Why can't your mom just stay with us while we're watching Daisy?"

"She can't leave her house full of foster kids for that long. You know that."

"I don't see why Terry should have to come all this way to get Daisy when she's really no trouble to us."

"It will just be better this way. Mom and Dad's life is all set up for kids. Ours is not."

His observation carries with it a certain sting, which I know is unintentional.

Doctors have always told me I would never have children. When I found out I was going blind, I realized that was God's way of solving a problem. Now, I'm not so sure what He's up to. I don't want to say God doesn't make sense. That would make no sense. That would be like a kid with some Tinker Toys telling Frank Lloyd Wright he's doing it wrong. Anyway, there are such things as blind mothers. I have looked up their organizations on the internet, and they are remarkable human beings. Now it will be my job to convince John of that.

"I'm sorry, Darling, if I have been insensitive," he says, picking up my hand. "I should have included you in this decision."

This is something he could not have managed to say, in a

way he could not have managed to say it, if he were in his depressed state. He would be the one taking offense, and I would be the one apologizing. His mood has swung toward the light ever since he announced his decision to send Daisy away. For this I should be grateful. But I am too busy being mystified to feel gratitude.

9

The Memory of Light

"I used to sit around and try to remember when and how I fell in love with him." Terry rocks slowly back and forth on our back porch glider. I hear metal rubbing on metal in a slow even rhythm. And her voice is slow and easy just like that. "And then it would come to me. The dates. The places. But not the feeling. I could never remember the feeling. And that's what I wanted. Desperately."

"I don't have to try to remember falling in love with John," I tell her. "I fall in love with him all over again on a somewhat regular basis."

"That's great." Terry sounds legitimately impressed, but I know it's not impressive. It's a roller coaster through a pitch black tunnel. Every once in a while there's a pinhole of light, and sometimes the pinhole grows larger and larger until it's finally large enough for us both to fit through. And there is that moment of sunlight and the wind on our face.

"Sounds like the kind of thing Lily and Frank used to share," says Terry. "Ah, the beauty of simple love. Seemed like it was ever new for them. They used to play tag together. Regularly. She was much faster than he was, but somehow he'd always end up catching her. Maybe because she always wanted to be caught. He'd swoop her into his arms and tickle her until she begged for mercy and then he'd press the world's longest kiss onto her cheek and she'd giggle and swat at him and tell him to stop and that he'd better run because now she's 'it.'"

I envy them. But I know games of tag aren't possible for me and John. As fun as they may be, they would make us miserable because they would be a reminder that we are not Frank and Lily. Life is not that simple for us. And yet I do wonder, if simple was possible for them, why not us. Why not anyone?

"John told me Lily suffered from depression. But never when she was with Frank, right?"

"You mean does love conquer all?" Terry stops rocking and looks into my face. "You're probably wondering why your love isn't enough for him."

"Yes. I could have sworn there was a time when I made him happy."

"Happy maybe. But not well. Love can't cure depression any more than it can cure the common cold. If you love someone, you will bring them chicken soup. You will fluff their pillows and make sure they have a steady supply of tissues. But none of that cures the cold. It just makes it easier to live through."

At first, I wonder how Terry knows all this. Maybe Jake suffers depression. I feel silly when I realize there was no mystery to any of this. She was John's mother. Her love couldn't cure him either.

"And then you might end up getting the cold too, you know," Terry says.

"Yes, I know that. I know it well."

"You've gotten it then?"

"When I let myself go where he goes."

"Into the dark, you mean.'

"Yes. But I don't know how to love him without following him where he goes. Can you love someone without feeling what they feel?"

"To love at all is to be vulnerable."

I nod.

"C.S. Lewis."

"To defeat the darkness out there," I say, "you must defeat the darkness inside yourself."

Terry nods.

"Hollywood's interpretation of C.S. Lewis."

"One of my favorite movies," she says, still nodding. "Hollywood got it right that time."

"So I am supposed to love him but not let him bring me into the dark."

"You might have to go into the dark. But bring light with you. In the moments you can. In the moments when you have light to bring. In those other moments, when it's too dark inside, just sit outside and wait. Patiently wait. The memory of the light will draw him out. He will come looking for it."

"I just don't understand the reason for the darkness. He says he doesn't know either."

"I remember Lily's psychologist—you know, Danny, the one who became a priest—I remember him once telling me that people come to him claiming they are depressed for no reason. But what they really mean is that they are depressed for a reason they haven't figured out yet or don't want to. He seemed to think depression has a cause and that cause could often be traced to something unforgiven."

"Really? I've never heard that before."

"That's what I understood him to say. And it is often one's

own unforgiven self. But I know that wouldn't have been the case with Lily. She forgave everything. And everyone. Including herself."

"Did she really ever need to be forgiven?"

"Oh yes. She had her moments, like we all do. It wasn't always easy living with Lily. Most of the time through no fault of her own, though. Sometimes just because she inspired or required you to do things you never would normally do. It was usually Jimmy who would get roped into her plans. I think he'd start out thinking it was going to be fun to help her out. One thing she'd make him do regularly is drive her go-kart. Lily's legs were too short to reach the pedals, so Jimmy would always have to drive, and she'd want to go again and again and again. You wouldn't think any boy would consider it drudgery to drive a go-kart. But he'd complain about his knees being all cooped up. I think he probably logged enough hours on those things that when it came time to get his license, driving was just second nature. It was always ever new to Lily, no matter how many times they went 'round. She would wave at everyone waiting their turn, at each and every lap, she'd be waving. Same people, and they'd all wave back. She even waved at the people painted on the wall."

"She loved everyone, huh?"

"Yes, pretty much. And most especially Jimmy."

"Which is why he could never say no to her."

"He never could. He'd get frustrated with her from time to time. But love fixes a multitude of problems."

"Can love fix John and me?"

"It's the only thing that can. If, indeed, it can."

"John strikes me as someone who is grieving. The mourning fog lifts on occasion, maybe when he has something to distract him, but it always returns at some point, sometimes thicker than others, sometimes too thick to even see through."

"It seems to me some people walk through grief, some people crawl and a few run," Terry says, bringing her glider to a halt. "Lily just seemed to sit down and let the grief wash over her."

"Lily weathered all the losses and came out Lily, except for the last one. She never fully recovered from the loss of Frank. She just stayed in their apartment for the longest time, sometimes sprawled out on their bed, crying into the mattress, wearing one of his shirts. Sometimes sitting on the couch hugging a bundle of sticks that were part of Frank's collection. Beth would come in and try to convince Lily to draw or paint or go help with the animals. Lily refused and cried even louder. She didn't take up her drawing again until Beth got a place with an art studio. The two of them would spend hours together painting. Beth had firsthand experience in how healing art could be. And it was really a service to humanity to have Lily painting again. The world needs to have Lily's artwork in it."

"Yes, we have several of her pieces."

"But you know, even after she started living her life again, there was still something Lily couldn't do. She could not eat pizza. Pizza is what Lily and Frank ate on their first date and on just about every day after that."

"So Pablo told Lily one day, 'don't you know you're supposed to eat the favorite food of your loved one? It is an honor to them when you do.'"

"I can- ea- pizza, Daddy. Not without Frank. He not here anymore to have his favorite things."

"But pizza is your favorite food too, Mija."

"Not any more."

"Aw now, how would Frank feel if he knew his moving on to heaven, where they have the best pizza in the world, robbed you of years and years of pizza?"

"I don- wanna live for years and years. Not without Frank.'

And I don't wanna eat pizza without Frank."

"Tell you what, Mija. Dia de Los Muertos is coming up. I wish I could fly out there and spend it with you. We would have a big celebration. But you can send me pictures. So this is what I want you to do. Are you ready? There's a lot to remember."

"No I can remember a lot, Daddy."

"That's OK. You'll remember this. I want you to go get a nice big blanket and a nice big pizza and some of Frank's other favorite foods and ask Terry or one of the girls to drive you out to Frank's grave. Then, walk right up and say, 'Hi Frank, I've missed you so much, and I've brought us a feast.' And then spread the blanket out and have a picnic. People have been doing that for years and years on Dia de los Muertos. You know what that is, Lily? That's called the day of the dead. All Souls Day. They say the smell of our loved one's favorite food goes right up to heaven and they actually get duplicates of whatever we eat down here. So, see? You can share your favorite foods with Frank again. And then while you're there, you clean up around the grave and leave some real pretty flowers, make the place look special."

Now it wasn't anywhere near All Souls Day when Pablo gave Lily this idea. But it wasn't long after that telephone call that the warm summer breeze, carrying the scent of fresh cut grass, made it the perfect day for two lovers to share a picnic. Perfect, if it hadn't been for the grounds keeper who drove up in his golf cart as soon as Lily got her blanket spread out on Frank's plot.

"We prefer you don't eat on the grounds, Miss," he said.

"I not Miss. I'm a Mrs. This is my husband." Lily pointed her thumb over her left shoulder at Frank's grave marker, which summed up the man this way: "Beloved Husband, Cherished Friend, Ringer of Bells, Collector of Sticks."

"Oh, OK, Mrs., sorry 'bout that. But maybe you could go eat over at the park. There's a nice ramada there and a duck pond."

"But Frank's not there, and I trying to share some of our favorite food with him. You wanna piece a pizza?"

"No, thanks. It's a real nice idea and everything. It's just that people tend to make a big mess when they bring food on the property. And all the bugs come too. And we just got rid of the bats."

"Bats like pizza?"

"No, they come at night to hunt for bugs."

"We won- make a mess. I promise. Here, have some pizza. Frank and me not gonna eat the whole thing. He used to be able to eat a whole pizza."

"Really? Frank's got my respect. I thought I was the only one who could do that." He patted his big belly.

This was all caught on home video, by the way. John had driven Lily to the cemetery and went for a walk in the neighborhood to give her some time alone with Frank. She had asked him to set up the camera on his tripod before he left so she could always remember her special time with Frank and so she could send a copy to Pablo and make him happy that she had followed his exact instructions.

"I have some American cheese too," Lily said to the caretaker. "Do you like cheese?"

It was becoming clearer and clearer to the gentleman that he was not going to get this persistent widow to leave.

"Tell ya what. I will take a piece to go. Then I'll leave you to be with your Honey. Three's a crowd and I got some work to do." He reached out his hand to accept the cheese and a smile grew under his heavy mustache. "Thank you kindly, Mrs., uh, Mrs. I'm sorry, you probably told me your name, but I got a terrible memory for names. Never forget a face, but names have never been my strong point."

"Mrs. Stillwell. I got the same name as Frank."

"Oh, of course! Dumb ol' Roger. What else would Frank's wife be called? Now his is a name I will never forget. Every time I pass by here, I say to myself, "Someday, I'm gonna find me a stick worth collecting, just like that Frank Stillwell fella. Then my loved ones will have something to put on my tombstone besides "eater of whole pizzas."

Lily smiled.

"Do you still have his stick collection?"

"Oh, yeah. 'Cept for the one he took with him. It was his favorite. Well, not his very first favorite, but the best one that fit in the box with him."

"And what about the bells?"

"The bells?"

"Says here he was a bell ringer."

"Oh, he don- keep the bell. It at church."

"He rang the bell like Quasi Moto?"

Lily burst into laughter. "No, no, silly. He a altar server."

"I used to be an altar boy too."

"Frank always rang the bell perfect. Everybody said that. Three long rings. Rinnnnnggg. Rinnnnggggg. Rinnnnngggg. And then exactly no noise. It quiet all around the Church. Only Frank could do it that good.

"Ah, I wish I coulda met 'im."

꘤꙰ꙮ꘤ꙮ꙰ꙮ꘤꙰ꙮ꘤꙰

I pour Terry some more coffee. "I wish it was as easy for all of us to make friends as it was for Lily," I say. "Seems like everyone automatically liked her."

"Yes, it was amazing. For the most part. Course you know there were a few people whose hearts were impenetrable, even to charms as captivating as Lily's."

Sometimes the doorbell would ring at the Greeley house, and there would be a neighbor with a complaint standing at the door. There was only one of her, but she seemed like a committee. It was the same neighbor suspected of reporting to the home owners' association that the garbage can, on occasion, stayed out a day too long. Actually, on quite a number of occasions. After Jack left her, Bev always resented the garbage. Not the stench or the weight of it or anything like that. She resented having to move it. The incentive of ridding her life of things that rot was enough to motivate her to get the garbage can to the curb. But returning the empty can to the backyard carried no such incentive. The only motivation was ensuring that they didn't put a lien on her house after issuing her a fine she had no intention of paying because she had a philosophical opposition to home owners' associations in general and one that is blind to the plight of single moms specifically.

It wasn't just trash cans. This neighbor found many things to occupy her time, a plethora of things to keep her unhappy. It was really only a matter of time before Lily would be blamed for a portion of that unhappiness. Apparently, it is quite unnerving to have a kid on monkey bars looking over the fence at your yard, and Lily had made a habit of doing just that. She had made friends with the Pittsbergers' yappy yorkies. Something about the way their back halves lifted off the ground when they barked made Lily laugh, and the more she laughed, the more they barked. The pair of overgrown caterpillars were, according to Bev, at least a hundred times more annoying than a kid could ever be, though not nearly as annoying as their owner. Bev nearly told her so, while she was standing right there on the Greeley doorstep, but a dose of sarcasm was more in order.

"Well, if those terriers of yours weren't such good conversationalists, it wouldn't be a problem. I know they talk a heck of a lot more than my Lily. So, maybe keeping them indoors more often would be the answer."

It was the first time anyone ever heard Aunt Bev say "*my* Lily." Bev was not a natural at motherhood. It was a calling she begrudgingly answered but did not choose. She inherited Lily, Terry and Jimmy when her sister died of cancer. She had no way of knowing that the life she so often railed against would, in the end, unleash upon her a torrent of unmitigated mercy.

"More coffee?" I ask Terry.

"Better not. Thank you."

Raindrops start to come down. They are big drops, spaced wide distances apart.

"What?" Terry says. "It actually rains here?"

"Never has before," I say. "Must be because you're here."

"Aw, you're funny. Maybe we better go in."

"If you want to, but we won't get wet. This is the kind of rain that comes straight down. It won't reach us under the porch."

"Wouldn't mind if it did," Terry says.

"Aw, you're homesick."

"Not one bit. Well, I guess I do miss my kids. And my Jake. But I'm enjoying my time here with you and John. And Daisy Grace. That little one." Terry's voice gets softer on those three words, and then there is pure quiet except for the splats of rain. For some reason, I start counting them. I get to thirty-two.

"There's no telling what kind of joy that little one is going to bring to this family," Terry says. "Being around her makes me miss Lily. Makes me miss my childhood with Lily."

"Really? What was it like?"

"Oh, it was wonderful. I can tell you, without a doubt, nobody else had one like it. And you know, it's still with me. I can't get through an hour, let alone a day, without thinking about Lily. Like every time it rains, I think of how Lily always insisted Auntie

Bev make it stop. No matter how many times she tried to explain no one has an on/off switch for precipitation, Lily was still always perturbed at Auntie Bev for letting it go on. Especially if it was accompanied by wind. But I think it was kind of a compliment. She didn't ask anyone else to turn off the rain. Not even Jimmy. She'd only ask Auntie Bev. Lily sure had a lot of faith in her."

୫୭ଽଈଽ୫୭ଽଈଽ୫ଽଈଽ୫୭ଽଈ

After Terry goes to bed, I decide it's time to tell John what it is his right to have known a number of weeks ago. Having his mother here will help the news go down easier, I think. I choose to wait until the lights go out, because hard things seem easier to talk about in the dark. It levels the playing field for me. I don't have to wish I could read his facial expressions because, even if I could see, I couldn't see. Even a sighted person has to guess at such things while lying in bed next to a spouse.

"I feel like if you could have kids, you would be happier," I say.

"You are more than enough for me, Charlotte."

"But I'm not. You are sad so often."

"It has nothing to do with you, Charlotte. Or with us. Or with our lack of children. I've been like this all my adult life. Having kids wouldn't change that."

"It could."

"No, Charlotte. You know that wouldn't be fair to a child. I can't take care of anyone else right now."

"You mean besides me."

"No, I mean besides myself. You do more taking care of me than I do of you."

"You know that's not true. And it never has been."

"You have no idea the good you do in my life, Charlotte. I don't know how I would live without you."

"I think we make a pretty good team. I'm not so sure why you have ruled children out of the picture."

"In my life, every happy thing has to be tinged with sadness. I don't have anything to give a child. A child deserves pure joy. Not that."

He has left me without a rebuttal. I will pretend to drift off to sleep.

10

Cheap Plastic Treasure

I am not usually one to accuse a cabby of driving too slow. I honestly can't tell you how fast he is actually going, since everything just moves outside the windows in a nondescript blur of white, beige and green. However fast it is, it's not fast enough.

John told me not to come, but I wasn't about to listen to him. He called from the emergency room and said he was in a minor accident on the way back from the airport to drop off Terry and Daisy. Something in his voice told me it wasn't minor. I knew he shouldn't have attempted to drive to the airport, but he insisted. He wanted to make it as convenient as possible for his mother, since I'm sure he felt he was already putting her out. He told me not to worry about coming to the ER since he was certain he would be released soon. They were just taking precautionary measures since he had hit his head. But he sounded shaken to me, and I know it is not good for him to be alone. I wish this cab ride would end. I can't tell where we are. I'm feeling car sick. Or baby sick. Or sick from the anxiety of not knowing what's happened to John, and how bad his injuries are, or how much emotional turmoil he might be in. We just had a conversation the other day about how much he hated driving.

"I don't know. I used to love it. I would beg my mother to let me go run errands for her. Sometimes I would intentionally forget something at the grocery store, so I could drive back again."

"Where was the first place you drove after getting your license?"

"St. Titus Church. Lily begged me to take her. She wanted to go to Confession, and my mother told her she would have to wait until Saturday, but Lily wouldn't hear of it. She insisted on going immediately to find a priest, and of course we didn't find one the first parish we went to, so she had me drive to five different parishes, which of course, I didn't mind at all. The more driving, the better. We finally found a priest in his office, who was able to squeeze in Lily's confession between appointments."

"Hmmm. I wonder what was so urgent about her need to confess."

"Well, that's no mystery. She told me all about it a number of times. Remember, we had upwards of two hours in the car together."

"So what was it?"

There was a gnat infestation in the Lovely home. Jake insisted it was the indoor jungle Terry had accumulated. She came home with a new houseplant just about every time she went to the grocery store. He tried to convince her the gnats were breeding in the soil. She refused to believe such theories and blamed it on the mangos he kept out on the counter to ripen. In any event, there was a computer in the kitchen that Lily liked to use for her artwork. She had a simple drawing and paint program that she would play around with. She didn't do anything serious on it. For her "professional" pieces she used actual oil on canvas or a mechanical pencil and paper or a ball point pen or colored pencils or watercolors. But when she simply wanted to relax, she would create art on the computer. Although it was a touch screen, Lily preferred the mouse. Drawing on a vertical screen requires you to hold your arm out for extended periods of time, which is too much like work. One day, during the height of the gnat infestation, Lily noticed random marks of yellow appearing on the screen, through no effort of her own. Her hand was resting on the mouse, but it wasn't moving. "Ghost!" she screamed. "Ghost! Ghost in the computer!"

"What are you talking about, Lily?" Terry came running. "What's wrong?"

"It painting! I not touching it, and it painting!"

Sure enough, swoops of yellow were making their way across the screen, while Lily's hands remained cupped over her mouth.

It just so happened that, at the moment the yellow line stopped, Lily dropped her hands and a gnat flew straight into her gaping mouth. She coughed and sputtered and spit until the gnat was expelled, or maybe swallowed, it was never clear.

Lily re-seated herself at the desk and went to put her hand on the mouse when it happened again. Another gnat charged at her face, then disappeared and the yellow line began again.

"A gnat is painting!" she exclaimed. "It not a ghost. It a gnat!"

Lily surmised that the gnats had figured out you didn't need a mouse to paint with the Lovely computer, just some tiny legs brushing across the screen. "They paint pretty good!" Lily appraised. "I think I let them paint more."

Lily immediately recognized artistic talent in the little prodigies. She knew they could do great things if only given the medium. So the next day, remembering that Terry always used vinegar as bait to attract gnats to fly paper, Lily wiped down the screen with white balsamic and then poured a small amount into the bottle lid and left it near the keyboard. This yielded the intended result of drawing a half dozen gnats, who, it turns out, were nesting in the soil of a nearby philodendron, and apparently felt a calling to a new, previously undiscovered artistic pass time. It was Lily's goal to let them create freely and then print the result and possibly sell it on ebay. She would call it, simply, "Gnats Paint." It did turn out lovely, and Lily was very pleased. But she didn't intend for the tiny artists to harass her indefinitely for days to come, every time she sat down at the computer. Despite washing down the vinegar, she spent more time shooing than painting and had a couple of very close calls in the left nostril. So somewhere around the tenth or eleventh day, she had finally had enough, and out of impulse and certainly not premeditation, she clapped her hands and killed one of them in mid-air.

She regretted it immediately upon seeing the lifeless black speck on her palm.

"So, she wanted desperately to go to Confession," John said.

"Because of a gnat?"

"I think she related to him because he was a fellow artist."

"I'm sure priests have heard pretty much everything, but I would have loved to be a fly on the wall in that confessional."

"Oh, to have that kind of faith."

"Why can't we?"

"I don't know. Maybe we can. If we could remember what faith is."

"How would Lily define it?"

"I don't know, but I do know that even she lost it for a little while."

Nobody ever knew why, but when she was a kid, Lily went through a short phase of lukewarm Catholicism. She wasn't hostile to the faith. She was complacent and lazy, and she complained every time she had to tear herself away from her Brady Bunch complete series boxed DVD set to attend Mass. She didn't want to put on her Sunday dress, then she didn't want to get her patent leather shoes on, and then, if it was raining, she didn't want to get wet. Seattle is not a good place for someone who doesn't want to get wet.

The whole protest would start with a question.

"Mass?"

"Yup, we're going to Mass."

"No Mass. I stay home."

"No we need to go to Mass, Lily."

"No Mass."

The Greeleys each took their turn trying to convince her of the merits of going to Church: you get to see your friends, you get to be in a nice peaceful, quiet place; you get to earn points toward your eternal reward; you get to be with Jesus and all the angels and saints; you get to eat donuts after.

None of that had any appeal, as much as she loved donuts, especially if they had pink icing and rainbow sprinkles, although she never ate that part. She would eat around it and leave it on her plate, refuse to throw it away and make Jimmy carry it around.

It was Jimmy who came up with a novel idea one Sunday morning, as Lily sat in the middle of the family room with her arms folded, refusing to put on her shoes. He decided to give her the simple truth as to why we go to Mass. "Jesus is sad when we don't go," he told her.

"Jesus sad?"

"Yes. He misses you when you don't go, Lily. He is happy when you come and visit Him."

"OK," she said. On went the shoes and off she went to the car.

After Communion, Lily looked at Jimmy with a big smile,

pointed to the crucifix and asked, "Jesus happy?"

"Yes," Jimmy whispered. "Jesus is happy."

ಬ⟫⟨ಣ⟫⟨ಬ⟫⟨ಣ⟫⟨ಬ⟫⟨ಣ⟫⟨ಬ⟫⟨ಣ

The cabby puts the taxi into park, so I assume we are finally at the hospital.

"Here you are, ma'am," he says.

"This is St. Joseph's?"

"Just like the sign says."

"Sorry, I can't make it out. Poor eyesight." I didn't want him to think I was illiterate, though why I cared about the opinion of a stranger whom I'd never see again, I'm not really sure.

"Sorry about that, Ma'am. That'll be twenty-four dollars."

"It's OK." I dig into my purse. Typically, I would have asked the dispatcher how much money it was going to be and prepared a roll of cash in advance. But I didn't think of it this time. It's been so long since I took a Taxi. I have become accustomed to John doing everything for me. I have forgotten how to survive on my own. "Uhm, would you mind helping me with figuring out the money here?" I stuff the contents of my wallet into his hand. "There's two twenties and a ten and a one."

"Actually, it's a five. Two twenties and a five. And a one."

"Do you have change? Can you take my two twenties and give me a ten?"

"Yeah, I can do that." He rustles into something in the front of the cab. "Here you go." He puts three bills back in my hand.

"Thank you." I shove the money in my purse and open the door.

"Do you need some help, ma'am?"

"No, I'm fine. Thank you."

I look out onto what I believe to be the hospital and see

nothing but blur. I realize it's going to be almost impossible to find my way in without running into someone or tripping and falling on my face. The last thing John needs is someone injured to take care of, if indeed he himself doesn't need to be taken care of. *Oh, Lord, please let him be OK.*

"Actually," I tell the cabby. "I could use some help. Could you just get me to the front door?"

"Sure, ma'am. You bet."

Turns out he stays with me the whole way, through reception and nurse's station, until I find John surrounded by curtains, lying on a gurney.

"Charlotte, Honey, I thought I told you not to come," he speaks into my hair, hugging me tight into him in a way I hadn't expected. He needs me here. Despite what he says. He needs me.

I turn to thank the cabby, but he is gone. I wish I had tipped him more.

"So, when you getting out of here?" I ask John. "What do the doctors say?"

"Still waiting on tests."

"Tests on what?"

"My head."

"Your head?"

"Yeah, it hit the window a couple of times."

"How? What happened?"

"Some guy turned left in front of me."

"At a light?"

"Yeah, the light turned yellow. I guess he thought I was going to stop."

"Is he OK?"

"Not sure."

"Well, what are they saying about your injuries?"

"It's just my head mainly. I lost consciousness a couple of

times, I guess."

"Lost consciousness?"

"Yeah, a couple of times."

"You didn't tell me that. You said you were OK."

"Well, I didn't want you to worry needlessly and rush over here."

"Like I did. Because I had a feeling you weren't being straight with me."

He picked up my hand. "I'm glad you didn't listen to me. I'm glad you came, Charlotte."

I smile at him and stroke his hair.

"Any news from Annabel?" he asks.

"No. None."

Turns out they want to keep John overnight for observation. He doesn't ask when and how I am going to get home, so I don't tell him I plan to stay the night. I call our neighbor to ask her to feed Little Sniff and let him outside. They put John in a private room on the third floor.

A man in khaki dress pants and aquamarine polo shirt pops his head in the door.

"Hello, anyone home?" His voice is melodic and smooth. He is in his mid-30s and wears his dark hair in short, soft curls that frame his round face. If you were to take a picture of him from the neck up, you would assume he was a chubby fellow. But he is actually quite efficiently built, with no excess of fat on his compact frame. As he steps into the room, it becomes clear that he is really all muscle.

"I'm Jim Roberts, the chaplain here. Mind if I visit for a sec?"

"Sure," John says, pushing himself up slightly in his bed.

"You must be John Lovely."

"Yes, I am."

"Pleased to meet you." The chaplain holds out his hand and the two men execute a handshake that reminds me of something you'd see on a retreat or revival weekend—firm and fraternal. The chaplain shifts his gaze to me and his brown eyes soften. "And how are you?" This time his handshake is gentle and genial, maybe even genteel, though not in a snobbish way.

"Just fine, and you?"

"Blessed."

"I'm Charlotte. I'm John's wife."

"Nice to make your acquaintance, Charlotte. And now where are you from? Do I detect a bit of the South?"

"A bit, I guess. And you too?"

"Yes, most people don't hear it anymore, but I'm originally from Atlanta."

"Ah. Pretty place."

"Yes, it is. So, John, I hear you were in a car accident."

"Yeah."

"Sorry to hear that. Probably not what you were expecting when you woke up this morning. But thank God you weren't hurt worse."

"Yes, it could have been a lot worse."

"Do you mind if we pray together?"

"Not at all," John says. "Can't hurt, that's for sure."

I make the sign of the cross, and I imagine the chaplain is folding his hands and bowing his head deeply as he emits a long and spontaneous prayer, which incorporates God's healing power, our names, John's skull and each hemisphere of his brain. Then he gives each of us a warm smile, and puts his hands into his pockets. He pulls his left hand out and is grasping something in his fist. He opens his hand and a string of blue beads cascades from his fingers.

"A priest friend of mine gave this to me. Said it belonged

to Mother Teresa. I guess this is the kind of beads she said her prayers on. These cheap, plastic ones. Nothing fancy. She wasn't into fancy, was she?"

"No," John says. "Definitely not."

"So, I would like to give this to you."

"To me?"

"I noticed when we prayed together that you crossed yourself. So I figured you must be Catholic. And I've always felt like these beads should belong to someone who is actually going to use them." Jim Roberts is still looking at the beads dangling from his hand. "I have prayed with a lot of people of all faiths, lots of them Catholic. And for some reason, I never felt called to give these away. I've been holding onto them for keepsake sake. You know, because they belonged to someone famous. But now, I hear God calling me to give them to you."

The rosary poured like liquid grace from the chaplains hand into John's.

"Wow. Thank you. But I couldn't. Really, I couldn't. You said you want to give them to someone who will use them. I can't promise I will. It's been a long time."

"You will use them someday. I'm sure of it."

"Well, thank you. I've heard about these rosary beads. She used to carry these around with her and hand them out to people. So, how did your priest friend end up with one?"

"I don't know. He said he had a number of them. I don't know where he got them. I'm assuming it's not something you can order on Amazon."

"No. I would think not. So why did he give it to you?"

"To tell the truth, I don't know. We used to have these long theological discussions. Maybe he thought it would do me some good." He winked and smiled again. "I've kept it for a long time because I happen to think Mother Teresa was an amazing lady, but

I am certain this one was meant for you."

When the chaplain leaves, I sit on the edge of John's bed. He places the rosary in my hand.

"You have a second-class relic of Mother Teresa," I tell him.

I sit for awhile watching one hand pour the beads slowly into the other. I begin a silent Hail Mary. It feels peaceful, so I say another. Then another and another. I haven't prayed a rosary in a number of years, but I have not forgotten. When I am done, I look over at John. I get close enough to his face to determine he has fallen asleep. I lay the rosary on his chest, kiss him on the cheek and realize there's nothing for me to do now but fall asleep in a chair. I hope they don't kick me out. The dread of riding in a cab at night makes it clear that I have lived a pampered life since I married John. I feel weak and anxious about being so dependent. I wonder if my neediness has contributed to John's depression. I feel a tightness in my throat as I think more about getting home on my own. My heart is pounding and I am feeling light-headed. How did I get to this place where I am so scared to be alone? My throat tightens even more, and I fear I will spiral into a full blown anxiety attack. My anxiety is causing me anxiety now. Yes, I understand how ridiculous it is, but I can't stop it. I am afraid of being afraid. I don't want to live in fear. I have learned that, nine times out of ten, fear is worse than the thing to be feared. But that doesn't help me right now. I consider begging them to let me share John's bed. I'm sure it would be against some rule or regulation. Section something, subsection so and so, paragraph whatever. Just as I have this thought, I hear a woman in the next room tell someone she has to leave because there are no visitors allowed between the hours of 10 p.m. and 7 a.m. I wonder what the sign says, if there is one. I wonder if it's weak and somewhat negotiable. Like maybe it says "Visitors encouraged to leave at 10 p.m." Or "Thank you for visiting between 10 p.m. and 7 a.m." If that were the case, I feel I could talk them out of it. Not like the sign at a ballfield near our house when I as growing up. *No dogs allowed on field. Sec 42-44 (c).* Now that one is clearly non-negotiable. It has the section numbers and letter to prove it. No one could say, "No, I am not sufficiently convinced that this is a legitimate city ordinance. I'm just going to let Rover play first base."

But I have a feeling hospitals don't bend rules, even if there are no subsections cited on the signs. I better get myself home and get some rest and get myself ready for a morning of nausea. Just one last time checking on John. Maybe he has woken up again and needs something.

I put my face next to his. He is still sleeping. I place my hand on his chest to see if Mother Teresa's rosary beads are still there. I feel them cascading out of John's hand. He must have found them there on his chest where I left them, maybe began to pray and fell asleep again. I will just go now and call a cab.

"Excuse me," I say to one of the nurses at the station. "Can you tell me how much money this is?" I put the three bills from my wallet up on the counter.

"It's three dollars."

"Three dollars? Are you sure?"

"Yes ma'am. Three. Three dollars."

Human nature is mystifying. What kind of person steals from a blind woman and then goes out of his way to see her safely to her destination? It's that strange mix of dark and light all rolled into one person that is always so difficult to understand. Like doctors who will risk their lives to care for highly contagious epidemic victims and then break quarantine. They were willing to die to save a patient, but not willing to stay home for two weeks and watch TV to save an entire population.

"Well, I know it's past visiting hours," I say. "But I don't have money for a cab. So, can I stay with my husband?"

"Oh, sure. Spouses can stay. Do you want me to try to find you a cot?"

"Oh, that would be perfect."

John is still sleeping when I return to the room, and I sit on the foot of his bed and listen to his heart beep on the monitor. It's a glorious, steady beat, and I am not taking it for granted. I could have lost him today. He could have died without knowing. It is wrong for me to keep it from him. He needs to know about his child. The sleep is probably good for him, but if he just happens to wake up, I will tell him.

The beeps are timed with my own heartbeat, at least in my mind, and for a minute I picture that John and I share one heart. It would be lovely that way. Easy. If only it could be.

ଓଝଔଝଓଝଔଝଓଝଔଝଓଝଔଝଓଝଔ

When the sun rises, John stirs. I am already awake. I am a bit nauseous and my back hurts from the lumpy cot. John is upset when I tell him about the cabby cheating me.

"What a rotten thing to do," he says, shaking his head. "How could anyone do such a thing? That kind of stuff used to happen to Lily. One time, someone traded her one bill for two by convincing her that two fives is bigger than a 20. What a rotten thing to do."

ଓଝଔ

11

Absent from Heaven

I never thought I would ever need to write a Dear John letter. It's hard to say goodbye. Especially when you are dead. But I'm writing this letter because ads for legacy boxes are plastered all over the hospital walls, and John spent forty-eight hours with nothing much to look at but hospital walls.

"It makes a lot of sense, Charlotte," he said. "Look how fast things can happen."

So he started gathering up paperwork—the car title, birth certificates, retirement funds—and putting it all in one drawer in the filing cabinet. I decided I would compose this letter, to be read after I die.

The words sound strange coming out of my mouth as I dictate to the computer. I can't believe I am dead.

Dear John,

If you are reading this, I have already passed to another place. I am still feeling your love for me. I hope you are still feeling mine. We are powerful like that, you and me. There was never anything lacking in the love that binds us together and there never will be.

I don't know what time of day it is right now. But I want you to go outside and look up. I want you to see the vast, endless, open, ongoing, uncontainable sky. I remember looking up at it when I was a kid. There were times I felt my soul expand to fill it. There were other times when it made me understand just how small we all are.

I felt that smallness in the times I was with you in the dark. I don't mean the kind of smallness you feel when you contemplate the vast infinity of stars. I mean the smallness you feel when there is nothing you can do to help the person you love most. I watched as you traversed your agony, or lay paralyzed in your grief. Know that I am still watching. Only now, I am not powerless to help. I will come to you, John, as soon as God allows. I will beg Him to let me hold your hand and walk with you. And I will lead you out. (I can see now, by the way,)

I can no longer suffer for you. I can only pray and guide and whisper things into your soul. I will whisper love to you, John There was a time when I suffered, but I wasted it. It wasn't until the end that I figured out what everyone is talking about when they say suffering is redemptive. God could have saved us in any other way than by suffering. But He had to show us how much He loved us. We wouldn't have understood if He just told us He loves us. He had to show us. That's how we are. So, He showed us how much our lack of love tortures Him. And then He showed us how much He was willing to endure to turn our hearts toward Him. And He would have endured much, much more. His suffering never did equal His love.

I don't want you to take this the wrong way. But it needs to be said. Being married to you made me suffer in all new ways. I suffered a lot in my life, but not out of love. It was useless suffering. It did nobody any good. I suffered because I had no other choice.

I could have suffered out of love for Him or love for you. But I resented my suffering and yours, wishing it could be taken away from us, not knowing that we had the power to turn it into a gift. There were those few times I got it right. I suffered for you. I suffered for love of you. And I have to say, in those times, it all felt different. It felt whole and redeemed, and somehow even right. It's not suffering that saves, but the love for which we suffer.

Do you remember the first time we met? You were this strong, (and I would learn later) handsome fella who could have been rubbing sun tan oil on some bikini-clad blonde. But you had given up part of your Sunday afternoon to bring Communion to a woman recovering from eye surgery. I'm sure I've told you before that I instantly loved you. A lot of people brought me Communion over the years, and I loved all of them instantly as well. But not like I loved you, John. How can I describe how much I loved you? I would have even eaten cake batter for you, even though I always said I wouldn't.

OK, well that about says it all, so I will sign off for now. But I won't leave your side, John. Not if I have anything to say about it. Try to know I am with you, John. Try.

I love you.
Charlotte.

The cake batter was an inside joke. John had told me once that Frank liked cake batter so much, that one year, Lily decided to give him an unbaked birthday cake. She found it a bit difficult to put the candles on, but after dipping little parfait bowls full of batter and serving their guests, Lily and Frank sat with the mixing bowl between them, licking big wooden spoons, and Frank said it was the best birthday cake he had ever eaten.

For me, it was the cake my Aunt Winnie made me on my eleventh birthday. It was a strawberry lemonade cake. At least that's what she called it. A lemon box cake with strawberry icing. Of course, when I grew up and learned how box cakes and ready-made frostings work, I realized it wasn't all that fancy. But it was the first cake anyone ever made me. Mama usually just put a candle in a Twinkie or a moon pie. The birthday girl got to choose. For my sixteenth birthday, my aunt came again. I asked her to make that strawberry lemonade cake again, and she said turning sixteen called for something a little more special. I was disappointed because I hadn't had that cake in five years, and I had been craving it all that time. But nothing my aunt ever did hurt my feelings. It's like she knew exactly how I felt all the time. Could she have been one of the very few adults in the world who remembered what it was like to be a kid? Well, I was not a bit disappointed when my aunt unveiled the strawberry margarita cake. It was the exact same cake, but with a swig of Tequila added to the cake mix prior to baking. It certainly was more special than my 11th birthday. But it was perfect because it tasted just the same.

I seal the letter and slip it into the legacy box. I can't believe I have failed to tell John the most important part of our legacy. Tonight will certainly be the night. Darkness or no darkness. Tunnel or open road. I can't keep this secret. I have asked a certain sister for help.

Ever since the accident, John has been spending hours on the computer. I feel bad for checking the history, but I can't help but think I need every clue I can get to how his mind works. All I came up with were searches for salt-free sunflower seeds in the shell, raptor rescues and Mother Teresa. He took an interest in her after trying to verify the authenticity of the rosary he was given. He googled to find out if the one he had was indeed the kind she gave away to people when she traveled. He concluded that it very well could be, but of course, there would be no way to prove it, since those little cheap plastic molded rosaries are made in large quantities by machines in China. In the final analysis, it doesn't really matter if John got an authentic Mother Teresa rosary or not. What matters is that someone spoke Mother Teresa's name into our lives.

While googling, John learned that she suffered from depression for decades—as a matter of fact, for as many decades as a rosary has.

I find this 1959 quote from her:

If I ever become a saint — I will surely be one of "darkness." I will continually be absent from heaven — to light the light of those in darkness on earth.

John isn't due home from work for more than an hour, so I decide to give the kitchen a good cleaning. I try to get the newest loaf of bread into the fridge so it won't mold, but there's no room. The Granny Smith apples need to be used up. I would make apple jelly, but John doesn't like me to use the stove anymore. Making preserves has been a specialty of mine for quite some time. Pretty much all southern girls can make jelly. We can't all can anymore. I certainly can't. So I just keep my preserves in the refrigerator. My mama could cook, but I didn't learn from her. She liked to fly solo. She wouldn't let me in the kitchen when she was in there. We took shifts. She would require me to make meals, but she would vacate the kitchen when I did. So, I am pretty much self taught. Except for preserves. She had me scrubbing baseboards one day and I made my way close to the kitchen and watched her measure out the ingredients for blueberry preserves — equal parts sugar and fruit and a splash of lemon juice. Scrubbing baseboards is what she made us do if she was mad at us for something small, like if we used two paper plates, stuck together, instead of making sure we only had one. She would tell us paper plates are 4.4 cents apiece and using two instead of one made it a ten-cent meal, not counting the food, (which probably cost less than the paper.) Mama would always buy the cheapest food and the most expensive brand of cigarettes and nail polish. Not the most expensive as in luxury brands, but the most expensive of the drug store brands. She claimed expensive nail polish actually saves money since the manicure lasts longer. She never really addressed the logic behind the expensive cigarettes. In fact, she never mentioned them at all, as if maybe the cloud of smoke engulfing her all day long would go unnoticed if she didn't bring it to anyone's attention. Not that she was at all coy. She didn't have to be. She didn't care what we thought. There was never a moment when she had to justify her actions. Going on the defensive would have given us some kind of power over her. And, believe me, we had none of that. No, those Davidoff Golds were never mentioned. When she was out of them, she simply said she was going to the store to get milk. She always did get milk, whether we needed it or not. Plus cigarettes, which she always needed.

As for me, I never have smoked, and John does the grocery shopping, so I don't have much of an excuse to leave the house. But the walls feel a bit close to me today. I have finished cleaning the kitchen, so I decide to go for a walk before John gets home.

I am summonsing my courage to tell what needs to be told. I make my way along the walkway, through the greenbelt that stretches out behind the rows of stucco. I remember on walks like this, when I was younger and had better vision, as the warm glow poured from people's windows, I would get a glimpse inside their homes. People were eating dinner, watching TV, cleaning their kitchens and I would think, "I wonder what their days hold. What exciting places have they been? What pains are they suffering? How complicated is it all to them? Their lives are so much simpler than mine, I am certain. So much happier. They have some kind of joy that never was mine to have and never will be. Or maybe there was some joy meant for me and I screwed it up somehow, and now I will never possess it. Other times, I would look into their brightly lit windows and see darkness. This, too, made me sad, because I was looking in there to find something I could hang some hope on. Even if it was someone else's coat rack. But I found nothing. That empty feeling of nothing.

John is waiting for me in the driveway when I get home.

"Where have you been? I've been going crazy with worry."

"I just went for a walk."

"By yourself?"

"Yes. By myself."

"Why?"

"I can still do it, John. I can still walk."

"Where did you go?"

"Just around the neighborhood."

"I just don't know why you would have gone alone."

"I went alone because I am alone. And I have been for quite some time. There's no one living in this place with me. This place where I am. I thought a walk would do me good. I was trying to connect to something. Someplace. And you know what? It didn't work. But I'm going to keep trying. My aunt used to quote Dag Hammarskjöld: *Pray that your loneliness may spur you into finding something to live for and great enough to die for.* Well, I haven't found it yet, but I'm going to keep looking."

"That's fine. Keep looking. But not by yourself."

"So, I can't ever be by myself again?"

"You make it sound so horrible."

"I don't get this, John. I'm the one going blind and I'm not allowed to be depressed."

And as if nothing I wrote in that letter has any truth to it at all, I go on: "You're so damn busy being depressed, and everyone else is so damn busy trying to keep you from sinking into a pit of despair, no one has time to feel their own depression. Well, I'm going to feel depressed now, OK? And you can walk on egg shells for awhile."

"You make it sound as if I have some sort of control over my depression, like I choose it because it's fun or something. Let me tell you something, Charlotte, it's no damn fun."

"And let me tell you something, John. You don't have to tell me. I know it's no damn fun. I live it with you everyday. Did you think you were in it alone, John? Yeah, you probably did. You don't see me there with you, John. You don't see me. Funny, I'm the blind one, but you're the one who can't see me."

"I told you before we were married, Charlotte. I warned you. This is how I am. I knew it, and you knew it. You said you would endure it all just to be with me. But you had no way of knowing. And I knew that. I knew you had no way of knowing. I knew you had no idea what you were getting into. But I wanted you. If I had been stronger, if I had loved you the way I should have, I would not have allowed it. I would have protected you. Nobody should have to live with this."

"I just don't understand. You hold it all together perfectly for everyone else. How come you have to be so different at home? Does going out there give you some kind of lift you can't get with me?"

"Quite the contrary. It exhausts me."

"Well, you don't look exhausted. Not until you get home."

"Look, the way I had always worked it before is if I didn't feel right, I didn't go out. I just stayed home alone and waited for it to pass. When I felt better, I'd resurface. So no one ever really knew the darkness I was in when I was home alone. Now there is no home alone."

"It's about me, isn't it?"

"What's about you?"

"Your regret. The irreversible choice you always talk

about, and you refuse to tell me what it is."

"You? Why would you come to that conclusion? I told you before we got married that I have wrestled with this thing for all my adult life."

"But not this bad, John. Not like this. It's about marrying me. Now you're stuck."

"No, Charlotte. No. Never. I will never regret marrying you. How can you even think that? That was the best decision I ever made."

"Really?"

"Really."

There was a long silence.

"Are you sorry?" he asks.

"Sorry? About what exactly?"

"That you married me?"

"No."

I am not going to tell him that there have been times when I would like to be released from the tunnel, and the realization comes that in my adult life before I married John, I never had to enter it, at least not for very long.

"You know, on second thought," John says, "maybe I am sorry I married you."

My throat tightens

"I don't want you to suffer because of me," he says. "I shouldn't have married anyone. Much less someone as good as you. You don't deserve this. Maybe I do. But you don't."

"What do you mean? How could you deserve to be miserable?"

"I don't know. I'm just not the nice guy you think I am. Remember I told you someone cheated Lily out of money once? Trading two fives for a twenty?"

"Yeah."

"That was Kip Daily. And guess who stood by and let him do it?"

"You?"

"Yes. Me."

"And that's why you deserve to be miserable?"

"Lily was never anything but good to me."

"And I'm sure she forgives you. And understands the foolish things we do in our youth. She would never hold that against you, John. I mean, when you're young, your friends are everything."

"Lily was everything. I should have realized that."

"It was a momentary lapse in judgement. We all have them. John, believe me when I tell you, I've never met anyone with a kinder heart than yours. Which is why—" I swallow hard. "I am so glad—" I take a breath. "I am so glad you are going to be the father of my baby."

"What? No, Charlotte, we've discussed this before—"

"There's nothing more to discuss, John."

"What do you mean?"

"You are going to be the father of my baby. The decision has been made. Not by us."

"What? Are you telling me—"

"I am pregnant."

John exhales heavily. "How is this fair to a kid?"

"Well, God must have thought it was a good idea. He must trust us."

"That's no kind of logic. Children are born to bad parents by the millions."

"Well, I don't intend to be a bad parent."

"Nor do I. But intentions are just intentions. They are not always what comes to pass.

"Why does it have to be this way, John? Why can't I be

like all the other women in the world who can't wait to tell their husbands they are having a baby? Why did I have to dread this moment? And worry so much about how you will react to this, how you will weather the added so-called stress? It's a baby, John. A reason to rejoice. Why are we acting as if I just received a cancer diagnosis?

"How long have you known and not told me? Why did you put it off."

"Because I knew you were going to react this way. I knew you couldn't let yourself be happy. Let me be happy. Let our baby be happy. You probably will treat him just like you treat me."

"Now you get my point."

"No, John. I'm sorry. I didn't mean that. You're going to be a great Dad. You'll see."

"Did you say *him*?"

"Yes. I did."

"Wait, how far along are you? How could you know that already?'

"The baby is due in October. And I just said *him* based on intuition."

"October? How could you keep this from me?"

"I knew telling you wasn't going to go well."

"You knew that. Based on what?"

"Reality."

"Reality. Right. Something you're it touch with and I'm not."

"Was I wrong?"

"Look, you can't fault me for having concerns about this, Charlotte. Parenthood isn't easy for anyone. Even in the most ideal of circumstances."

"There is no such thing as ideal circumstances."

"Come on, Charlotte. You can't even pick a package of

tortillas that hasn't been tampered with."

"You're still mad at me for that?"

"I'm not mad at you."

"You are. You pretended to be angry with the store. But I could tell you were mad at me. You were mad at me that I didn't see the package was opened. That I can't even grocery shop any more. That you're going to be doing everything. And you were mad that I didn't know the cabby ripped me off."

"No, I wasn't mad at you, Charlotte. I wasn't. I know it's not your fault. I wouldn't be mad at you for that. I'm not an ogre, Charlotte."

"That's right, John. Now you've hit on the truth. You're not an ogre. It's time to stop treating yourself like one."

John's phone rings. It's Annabel. Jimmy and Georgia have been released from jail. They were cleared of charges of drug smuggling when they were finally able to convince authorities they had nothing to do with the transporting of drugs from South America, through Mexico, to the United States. They had just happened to choose a seat that had cocaine strapped to the bottom of it at a time when officials were staging a raid of the bus.

Annabel also wanted to know if John had given any more thought to Marty's offer. He wanted John to move out to Boston and run one of the homes he and Annabel had set up for people with disabilities.

"You never told me," I say.

"I never gave it any serious thought."

"Why not?"

"Takes a special person to work with special people," he says, putting his phone in his pocket. "I don't think I've got it in me."

෫○✄ଓ

12

The New Normal

I awake to roses on my night stand. A dozen red. No special occasion. None beyond guilt, anyway. They are peace-offering flowers. They should be white. That's the color of peace and reconciliation. I know I should be happy to be getting them, no matter their hue. I just wish they were honest. Red is the color of love. And you can't profess to love me without loving the person growing within me.

I am settling in to something different now. Miserable is the new normal. Any moment that isn't misery is pure gift. I can't claim it. I can't orchestrate it. I can't hope for it. It just comes every once in a while. When it comes, it comes, and it is like a moment's relief from an excruciating toothache. I can't hope for it because hope hurts. It is far less painful to want nothing.

I move the roses into the kitchen. They are heavy in their weighty vase. I scuff instead of walk, just in case there are any foreign objects in my path, like a flip-flop or a little French bulldog, though Little Sniff usually knows to get out of my way. I hold the roses in close, and I feel my skin might turn to velvet, just by having them brush against my cheek. The smell of beauty cuts sharp and deep, and I am in the warm sunshine of the South, cutting roses for the table at the direction of my aunt, who is inside preparing for the tea. Tea was not just a beverage for my aunt and her friends. Tea was an event. They took turns hosting, and I was always invited when I was in town. I always had the most fun when it was my aunt's turn to host. I loved watching her in action. She had ample amounts of the classic Southern charms mixed with just a little crazy. I loved the crazy. It was the one thing that could make me forget.

I always found it interesting how different my aunt's friends were from her. And from each other. There was one other that had a little crazy mixed into her too. But the rest were just ordinary. One was a quiet introvert, who did little interacting beyond a faint smile. You got the impression she came to tea because someone in her life suggested it would be good for her to get out once in a while. She sipped her tea uncomfortably and nibbled daintily on her de-crusted cucumber and butter finger sandwich, waiting for tea to end so she could go home and pet her cat. It was my aunt's teas that fostered in me a warm appreciation for the under-appreciated introvert, because also in attendance at these events was the female version of General Patton. Her words came barreling into your face like a cannonball, and your natural inclination was, of course, to back up. The problem is that her natural inclination was to take a step forward. And this would go on for as long as the conversation lasted, or until your heels were against a baseboard or until someone mentioned it was time to be seated at the table. And then that woman with the voice of a chain-smoking coal miner would sit and raise her pinky and sip tea like Princess Grace. But you know, she gave my aunt the most amazing eulogy. And so, it was at my aunt's funeral that I learned to love that woman and appreciate all over-bearing women from that day forward.

I said earlier that I don't hope, but that's not exactly true.

I am harboring a bit of hope about the roses. Maybe they mean John will come home in a good mood. There are so many things I need to discuss with him, so many plans we need to make. Topics that will require him to be in a good mood. I decide to sift through the mail, putting each envelope up to my nose to read it, hoping to find good news that might be waiting for him when he gets home.

I put my face to the roses and study the veins in the pedals. My nearsightedness has progressed to the point that my eyes have turned into microscopes. I can't see anything past an inch of my nose, but anything closer than that I see in intricate detail.

The roses refuse to tell me anything. Do I dare hope that John will be coming home happy? Even if he left that way this morning, what are the chances that happiness as fragile as his could have endured an eight-hour day?

I hear the garage door, but no sign of John for several minutes. It's Tuesday, and tomorrow is garbage day. He must be putting the black garbage can at the curb. Probably not a good sign. He doesn't expect to be up early enough to beat the garbage truck, which means he is tired and uninspired. I will steer away from difficult topics and find something easy. I know how popular John was in high school, so I thought this one might fit the bill.

"Looks like your reunion is coming up," I say handing him the mail.

"Hmm." I hear him sorting through the envelopes, shuffling each one to the bottom of the pile after a quick pause.

"Are you going to go?"

"Heck no."

"How come?"

"No desire. Eddie is the only one I've kept in touch with, and I have no desire to change that."

"Didn't you like high school?"

"Does anyone really like high school?"

"I mean the experience. As a whole."

"Not really. It kind of stank."

"I thought you had a lot of friends?"

"Quite a few people I called friends."

"But..."

"But, Eddie was my only true friend."

"Maybe you should see if he's going to the reunion."

"You really want to go on a trip?"

"We haven't been anywhere for so long. Plus, we'd get to visit your folks."

"We can do that any time. We don't need a high school reunion for that."

"We can? We can do it anytime?"

"Sure. We'll plan it."

"When should we go? Should we go this summer?"

"We'll have to make a plan." And that, of course, means no.

"Oh, they called today about the altar linens," I say.

"What?"

"They wanted to know if you wanted to get back into the ministry."

"Wow. It's been so long. Why are they calling now?"

"I don't know. Do you think you might do it?"

"There's just a lot going on here, Charlotte."

"Yeah."

The very first time I came to John's house, he drew my attention to the Gardenia bushes that stood on either side of the walkway leading up to the porch. "Did you notice this one is twice as big as the other?" he asked. "That's because this is the one that receives Jesus." He broke off a fragrant white flower and handed it to me. "This is where I pour the water after washing the altar linens."

The linens are sent home with a trained volunteer and have to be washed in a large pan of water, which then has to be poured into the ground. This assures that any remnants of the Blessed Sacrament that might unintentionally be left on the cloths used in the consecration during the Mass will be returned to the ground. The process is repeated twice before the linens are then laundered in the washing machine. John had been on altar linen duty for years. It's usually old ladies who take it on, but John loves to iron. He says there's something soothing about it. I can't say that I agree. Even back when I could somewhat see, I found ironing to be the perfect mix of boredom and frustration. I ironed far more wrinkles in than I ever got out.

"I see you got the roses," John says.

"Oh yes. Thank you. They are beautiful. Where did you get roses so early in the morning?"

"I've got my sources."

John gets me flowers on occasion because I once told him people will probably stop giving me bouquets. If indeed they ever did. What's the sense in giving a thing of beauty to a blind person?

"I'm really sorry the words didn't come out right last night," he says. "And in the past four years. I'm just not sure how this whole baby thing is going to work."

I put my arms around his waist and lean into his chest. He strokes my hair, and I feel safe again.

"We'll figure it out," I say softly.

"Well, Mother Teresa used to say 'God will not give you more than you can handle.'"

"I've heard that before. A number of times."

"And then she would add, 'I just wish God didn't trust me so much.'"

"We're going to do this thing," I say. "Better than either one of us thought we ever could. We're going to surprise each other. You'll see. You'll see, my love."

৪৩✄ଓ

13

Ecological Atrocities

Shortly after the high school reunion, which John did not attend, he got word that Eddie died in a car accident.

"Edward was rare," John said softly. "He was a nicer guy than I can ever hope to be."

"Must be pretty darn nice then."

"He was great. He was my one truly decent friend. I wish I had gotten the chance to tell him so. I need to go to the funeral."

"By yourself?"

"Would you want to come?"

"Of course."

"OK. I just know you haven't been feeling well. I wouldn't want you to have to travel right now if you're not feeling up to it."

"I am. I want to go. Besides, we can see your family."

"Oh, no, the funeral isn't in Seattle. It's in L.A. That's where he ended up."

"Oh, well, that will be a nice trip too. And much closer."

"We won't even have to spend the night. We'll just do a turnaround."

The flight to Los Angeles is uneventful, except for the overly-curious elderly lady next to John. She gets him to talk. I probably couldn't have. It is good because the conversation takes my mind off of the big question: What good does it do to give the blind passenger the window seat? I wish I could see out. I would love to see the golden rays of evening pouring onto the top side of the clouds. Not that clouds are all that different from the top or from the bottom, probably. But being above them is, let's face it, wholly unnatural and exhilarating—or at least it should be.

John tells the lady all about Eddie. The best thing about him was his expansive smile. It was the best thing about him because it was a reflection of his over-sized heart. He tells her how kind Eddie always was to his aunt Lily. The lady wants to know exactly what Down syndrome is. She doesn't think she has ever met anyone who "is syndrome" as she puts it, though she has known people who are "not quite right." What was it like to live with someone like that? How much can they really understand?

"It might have taken her a little longer to get something, but once she got it," he tells her in his soft-spoken way, " it wasn't going anywhere. She never forgot the important stuff. Her hamster found his way into her prayers on the very first night she got him. And his death three years later changed nothing. She kept right on praying for him years after he was already gone. His name was always among the long list of loved ones in her nightly litany. Maybe she thought God was a bit forgetful because she would always start with the reminder that Timothy Sniff had died."

The lady seems unimpressed by this.

"Oh, I don't like rodents," she says. "That's why I like cats. They eat rodents. No offense to your syndrome aunt and her little mouse."

Lily always said she hated cats. Until she saw one in the driveway or at the park or on the backyard fence. She wanted to pet every cat she saw. So, in actuality, she really just disliked the idea of cats, but was quite fond of cats in the microcosm. I guess you could say the same for people who dislike Down syndrome. Eradicating it seems like a good idea, until you get to know someone who has it.

Although, strident environmentalists would probably prefer a world without the likes of Lily.

It took a while for Bev to understand why it was always necessary to make extra trips to the store for toilet paper. It was true she and Jack had more than doubled their household when they inherited Jen's three kids. So it made sense that everything they bought had to be multiplied by two.

But the need for toilet paper seemed to increase ten-fold. At first, Bev just figured Jen had trained her kids to aspire to overly-clean behinds.

"Am I going to have to take a second job just to bank roll the wiping of your fannies?" she'd grumble as she grabbed her purse and keys and coupon clutch and headed out the door. She would always ask the neighbors to save the toilet paper coupons for her. In exchange, she'd give them any other coupon they wanted, even buy-one-get-one-free gourmet coffees.

Then, one day, the discovery of something quite unexpected cleared up the mystery of the highly unusual per capita toilet paper consumption in the Greeley household.

While looking for one of Lily's sandals under the girl's bed, Bev found a Hello Kitty rolling suitcase full of toilet paper rolls, picked fully clean of all toilet paper, including those little shreds that always stick to the two stripes of glue laid by the factory.

"What are all these?" Bev asked Lily. "Where's the toilet paper that was on all these?"

Next to the Hello Kitty suitcase was a basket of toilet paper rolls cut in half. Next to that was a bag with some scissors, art pencils, tape and glue. Next to that was a shoe box full of papers, each of which had a butterfly emblazoned on it with wings drawn in colored pencil and a body made of a half toilet paper roll.

Bev moved stuff around under the bed, hoping to find a stash of toilet paper that corresponded to the cardboard rolls. "Where's the toilet paper, Lily?"

Now most kids, at this point, would have felt pangs of guilt, and most likely even waves of fear. But Lily simply took Bev by the hand, led her to the bathroom and pointed into the toilet.

"You flushed all the toilet paper down the toilet?" Bev asked.

"Yeah."

Although Lily loved wild animals, she had no compassion for the rest of the ecosystem. She lived as if she held a deep disdain for the world's rainforests.

She would ruin reams of paper by drawing one large circle in the middle of each sheet and leaving it in the discard pile. Everyone figured she was practicing her drawing and when the picture started with an imperfect circle, she would simply get another sheet and start over. Apparently, she hadn't heard of the history-altering invention—beloved by artists and mathematicians alike—called the eraser.

Lily also seemed to make it her life's ambition to squander nonrenewable resources. This would entail playing with the thermostat, right before the Greeleys left for a week-long winter vacation, so the house would be heated to ninety-six degrees the whole time they were away. Or turning the air conditioning down to sixty-two right before bed on a hot summer night.

Lily lived her life as if she owned stock in General Electric. Every night after everyone had gone to sleep, she would awaken and turn on every light in the house. Bev would wake up in the middle of the night to wattage rivaling that of a baseball stadium.

She'd turn off all the lights and find them all on again the next morning. The only workable solution was to go around the house every night before bed and give the light bulbs a quarter turn. Would have been the perfect solution. But everyone else in the house complained they had to stumble around in the dark if they had to get up to use the rest room or blow their noses or get a drink of water.

While these stories are recounted frequently in family folklore, these were among the things John did not tell our fellow passenger about living with people like Lily. She was still talking about the superiority of cats over other companion animals.

ಏ❧ಬ❦ಏ❧ಬ❦ಏ❧ಬ❦ಏ❧ಬ❦ಏ❧ಬ

The funeral is typical for someone who dies suddenly at an early age. Everyone is too shocked to be reflective and grateful. That will come later. For now, there is no comfort, no thoughts of death being a relief or a passage. "He's in a better place" rings hollow and cliché.

"I don't understand it, Charlotte," John says on the flight back home. "Why is Eddie dead?"

"At such an early age, you mean?"

"I could never hope to be even half the man he was. Why would God take him from this earth, where he could have done so much good, and leave behind a loser like me?"

"You have a great deal of good to do, John. You know that. You're just being silly now."

"No. Eddie was a great guy. I mean a great guy."

"You're a great guy too. That's why someone great like me married you."

"I thought it was my dashing good looks."

If Aunt Winnie could have met John, I know exactly what

120

she would have said. She would have hugged him tight, looked at me and said "Well, ain't he perty." She would have reminded the two of us each time we saw her how "perty" he is. She would have called him her boyfriend. And it wouldn't have mattered whether he was "perty" or not (though I must say, he is quite perty). That's the way it would have gone. And both John and I would have felt loved by it all.

There were a number of sayings about beauty when I was growing up, all of which seemed to contradict each other, but they would all be used to prove what ever point was necessary to prove at the moment. *Pretty feathers make a pretty bird. Beauty is only skin deep. Pretty is as pretty does.*

You could sum up my childhood by saying it was all just one long string of contradictions. Was I beautiful or hideous? My aunt told me one thing and my mama another. Who was the more reliable source? And did my parents love each other or loath each other? She would sit on his lap and he would have his hand wedged into her jean pocket and she would laugh at his jokes. Then, before you knew it, she would be throwing his beer bottle across the double-wide. Fortunately, it rarely hit anybody. It grazed the cat once, but did no damage. Not physically anyway. That cat was already neurotic. Mama had it in for her because she wasn't a dog—a specific dog named Bernie. Bernie was a cow dog, and she was my mama's favorite living being. And it was not a good day when Daddy backed over Bernie with his Ford pickup. Mama beat his chest for over ninety seconds and didn't talk to him for a month. I have a vague memory of watching Daddy dig a hole in the backyard and then another vague memory of watching out the window as Mama knelt by the mound of fresh dirt there and cried. Daddy drank a beer in front of the T.V. while that was going on.

I stood there wondering if she would carry on over me like that, if I were to die. I had a hard time picturing it.

I did inherit my mama's love of dogs. If there is anything good about going blind, it's that you can have a service dog. I am on the waiting list, and I know we're going to be good friends. For now, I've got Little Sniff, who is not exactly useful, but very charming. John found him wandering in the park one day, and no one ever claimed him.

John finds a lot of animals in the park, and if they are sick or wounded, he usually brings them to me. He says I have a gift. He says this because one time we were actually able to release into the suburban wild a sparrow that I had nursed back to health after John found it flitting in some rushes unable to fly. I'm not sure what went right with that one because the multitude of other poor unfortunate creatures he has brought home in cardboard boxes have succumbed to death inside the box, amongst the fistful of grass, small heap of seeds, a helping of dead cricket and bottle lid filled with water. The poor things probably died more prematurely than if John had left them alone to take their chances as easy prey. I know it sounds ridiculous, but I cry over each one. I really can't help it. It takes me by surprise every time.

Apparently, Lily had the same "gift" I do—the gift not so much of healing animals, but the gift of wanting so very badly to heal animals. One time they found that Lily had been harboring a wounded bird in her closet for quite a number of days. It was never determined exactly how long, but there was no shortage of droppings in the suitcase where she had laid him on a bed of sport socks after binding his broken wing with a Little Mermaid band-aid.

Lily would have made a wonderful mother. Since she never had children of her own, John filled that empty spot for her. He was conceived with her in mind. Sounds strange, I know, and maybe even wrong on some level, but Terry wanted to give her sister the opportunity to help raise another human being, so she went to great lengths to have John. And Lily did, indeed, cherish him as if he were hers.

"This is our baby's first flight," I tell John, just after a round of turbulence sends shock waves through my belly. "I wonder what it feels like in the womb when a plane jumps over an air pocket."

"Don't know." I assume he is still engrossed in his in-flight magazine. His response makes me feel like I've said something wrong, so I return to observing silence about the person growing inside me. The remainder of the flight is quiet. The lady from the outbound flight is not here to make John talk.

I decide to cook when we get home. John loves Mexican food, so I know he will like this recipe for taco soup I find online. We don't have Mexican style stewed tomatoes, so I use diced tomatoes and a can of green chiles instead. And we don't have Monterey Jack, so I use cheddar. I substitute dehydrated onions for a fresh one, since I can avoid using a knife. It all turns out pretty darn good. Whenever my aunt used to get complimented on a meal, she'd say "I've got me a red-hot can opener." And she'd add, "People have a hard time believing that cuz everything I make tastes like I fussed all day." Then she'd smile and point her finger right at your face and say, "But I didn't." The secret was in how she "doctored" it. In most cases, that was code for extra butter and/or extra sugar and/or a generous amount of salt and pepper.

I am hoping the soup will put John in a good mood. Maybe we can even daydream together about what it will be like to have a baby.

"Good soup," he says.

"Thank you."

"Very good."

I decide the baby topic might ruin things. I realize there's never an optimum time to broach sensitive subjects. When things are going well, you don't want to spoil it. When things are not going well, you have no hope of a successful discussion. How I come up with the next question, I do not know. I guess I thought it would be easier talking about his past than our future.

"Do you ever talk to her?"

"Who?"

"Lily."

"What do you mean?"

"I mean like you would talk to your patron saint."

"Not sure either one of them would listen to me at this point."

"What makes you say that? Don't you believe the veil can be lifted?"

"Yes, I believe that. I just don't know why Lily would want to talk to me."

"You know, you paint a much different picture of Lily than everyone else in your family."

"No. I'm not trying to paint a picture of Lily. The picture is of me. It's not a pretty one."

"There couldn't be anything ugly about a picture of you, John. But something's not right between you and Lily. What is it?"

"I've told you before. Lily loved me, but it didn't count. She didn't know what I did to her. I was debating whether I should tell her. And then suddenly it was too late."

"What did you do to her?"

"I can't talk about that, Charlotte. I just can't."

"OK. Fair enough. But you can't hold it against yourself forever. Lily would not have understood that. She would not have understood grudge holding. She certainly wouldn't have condoned it. Grudges are in the past. That's not where Lily spent her time, is it?"

"I never got a chance to apologize to her. I kept debating, wondering if I should tell her, thinking I had time to decide. One day, I was out of options. Lily was gone and that put an end to the possibility of ever asking her forgiveness."

"And what would she have said if you had asked her?"

"She would have forgiven me."

"Then can't you just consider it done?"

"Without hearing it from her? How would a person do that?"

"I don't know, but I know it's been done throughout human history. I know that's what people have to do. How many people have everything resolved when a loved one dies? Who in this world has said everything they need to say?"

14

Habanero Jubilee

Lily had a way of bringing out the best in people. Even Las Cocineras Bonitas, a trio of restaurateurs whose tempers were as fiery as their food. Their customer service bordered on abuse. But no one went there for the warm fuzzies. They went for the heat. There was no other place in Seattle that used the amount of habanero peppers that Las did, so they could get away with treating their customers with deep disdain.

People came to Las because they desired, craved, required and longed for hot food. They would do anything, withstand anything, endure anything and put up with anything to get it. So it was not advisable and never in your best interest to get yourself kicked out for rude behavior or let your indignation get the best of you and storm out offended. Customers who did this would only have to return, slinking through the door with heads hung low, humble and repentant, stewing in their remorse.

The place was virtually always packed, despite the fact that all the staff, from management down to the bus boys, did their best to make it clear that they resented having to serve you.

Unless you were Lily. Lily's arrival was like a Jubilee, a time in which mercy would be shown to all customers. I will get to the details on that in a minute. But first, you need to understand how the place ran on days she did not come.

There were overt as well as unspoken rules, and occasionally there were customers who would break them. Maybe they were novices or maybe just slow learners or maybe just foolish people whose pride out-swelled their craving for hot food. But the smart customers knew no good could ever come from challenging or breaking the following rules:

Rule No. 1: Don't ask for substitutions, like "can I have whole beans instead of refried on the enchilada platter?" It says right on the menu, *NO SUBSTITUTIONS!* Learn to read, for Heaven's sake.

Rule No. 2: Don't be high maintenance. Questions such as, "Can I have my rice on a separate plate?" or "May I have a refill on my Coke?" or "Could we get some more chips and salsa?" will not be tolerated. If it comes to you, you may have it, but do not request it.

Rule No. 3: Don't ask for special accommodations, such as, "Since it's 97 degrees and 90 percent humidity, can we just wait inside until the ninth person in our party arrives?" You know darn well it is the policy for you to wait on the patio and order overpriced margaritas and pay for bowls of chips until your entire party has arrived. Record heat or no record heat.

Rule No. 4: Don't ask stupid questions, such as "What would you think if I just took my business elsewhere?" or "Do you even care if we stay or go?" You will not like the answer and then you will find yourself in the awkward and unenviable position of eating crow before your chips and salsa even arrive.

Rule No. 5: Do not threaten to give them a bad online review. They will bring the laptop to your table and boot it up for you. And after your review is posted you will be banned from Las Cocineras Bonitas forever.

Rule No. 6: (This may be the most important and one that should go without saying, but believe it or not, there have been customers who dare to ask.) DO NOT ASK IF YOU CAN HAVE YOUR FOOD MILD. Those tacky warning signs reading "You're gonna get burned!" and ugly caricatures with their tongues on fire, printed on those bright orange letter-sized paper, curling at the corners and stained with salsa, are posted at every booth for a reason. Asking for your food mild is the equivalent of asking the Pope to ordain women.

Aside from that one, there are exceptions to every rule. Even at Las. But the exceptions only ever applied to one person and, for the most part, those in her presence. If you wanted to be treated like anything other than pond scum, you had to be dining with or around Lily. If the Lovelys called ahead, Las Cocineras Bonitas would even put the "Lily Special" up on the blackboard, so it would be waiting for her when she walked in.

The Lily special was simply a very large tortilla, sprinkled with a hearty helping of Manchego and Queso Blanco, passed under the broiler until bubbly. It was virtually the only thing in the restaurant that did not cause a three-alarm fire on your tongue. And if it didn't happen to be a night when Lily was coming, it simply could not be had.

I am thinking about all of this, and the way the Lovelys retold the story, as John and I sit out on the patio of a Mexican restaurant where the service is fabulous, and it has to be, because the food is not worth suffering any emotional abuse.

We are here because last night's taco soup made us both crave tacos and Baja Baja's is right around the corner from our house. There's a nice heavy feeling to the air and I think there must be a spectacular sunset.

"John, will you tell me about the sky?"

"What?"

"Will you tell me what the sunset looks like right now?"

"Just a typical evening sky. Nothing spectacular."

"Describe it for me."

"I can't really. It's just an evening sky."

"I would love to hear about it."

"Haven't I described it for you before? A number of times?"

"Yes, you have. And it was beautiful. Remember, when we first came to Arizona? We would drive out to South Mountain, hit that vending machine at that resort and grab us a couple of cans of orange juice with honey and sip on them while we watched the sunset. And you would tell me what the clouds were doing."

"I'm sorry, Charlotte. I'm afraid I am not feeling too poetic about the sky right now."

I know he is worried about being a father. But I don't want to have that conversation right now.

"Well, I wrote it down. Most of what you told me then about the sky. All the beautiful things you said. Maybe you can read it to me when we get home."

"Really, Charlotte, I'm sorry. I am just not in the frame of mind."

"Not in the frame of mind" means he wants to be left alone. Or at least that's the way I always interpret it. So, I just leave him alone. Sometimes for days. On those days, I will read and re-read what I wrote on the days when he loved me. So that's what I do when we get home from Baja Baja's. I get right under the lamp and put the paper at my nose and read, while John sits in front of a nature documentary about those shrimp that have six eyes and a left hook that can do the damage of a 22-caliber bullet.

The sky is a bowl turned upside down. The sherbert has melted into swirls. Somehow, it all stays. Gravity apparently has

129

no power over sherbet. Or maybe it has coated the bowl in just the right amount. There is no excess there, nothing to fall. The raspberry and orange troposphere has cured onto the glass, and even the wisps of cirrus pineapple somehow adhere to the dome.

And then, as if it is written right there on the paper, these words enter right into my brain:

There is always something ridiculous about the emotions of people whom one has ceased to love. It's a quote from Oscar Wilde's *Picture of Dorian Gray.*

And I know now, in this disheartened moment, that I am ridiculous, and I know exactly why.

15

The Fork in the Drawer

We don't see the mountains from our house, but John tells me we can see them when we drive somewhere. He says they are straight down at the end of the road we take to Ikea. I guess they rise up out of nothing. To me, that's what this whole city seems to do. As much as there is here to take your mind off the desert, it's not hard to imagine a time when there was nothing but Saguaros and chollas and ocotillos, and scaly-skinned critters that rustle through dry brush and disappear into holes and crevices. I am glad the mountains are there. Even if they are not visible from the house, at least when we are driving, we know the road doesn't stretch on forever. I don't know why that would be disturbing to me. Maybe because I am from the south. In the south the road is bound to end somewhere. Most likely, it turns to dirt and ends in front of some saggy porch with a creaky glider. What I wouldn't give to sit in one of those right now, and just push back and forth, back and forth, and think of nothing. The creaking scrapes the mind clean somehow. My mind needs a good scraping. I don't have a whole lot to be nostalgic about, but the thought of that glider makes me want to go back to a simpler time. It wasn't joyful, but it was simpler.

My Aunt Winnie once told me something that I never forgot. She told me there was a God and that He loved me. So, I would think about Him constantly, and I am quite certain that those thoughts were the only thing that saved me. Those thoughts and maybe that fork in our drawer. Somehow one of my aunt's forks made its way to our house. Maybe we brought it home in a casserole after a wake or maybe she brought it into our house in one of her salads. She used to make the most amazing salads. They were even impressive to a kid, and you know kids don't usually offer praise and adulation to vegetables. But my aunt would bring one every time she came, which wasn't often enough. And the thing would look like a Robert Delaunay painting, passionate with color and geometry. Like the clothes she would wear—large flowing fabrics riddled with over-sized triangles and circles or tropical flowers. She'd always have something interesting from the opposite side of the color wheel hanging from her ears.

I'm not saying I would gobble up my aunt's salads, but I would always dip some on my plate. You couldn't walk by it. It was a thing of beauty and you had to possess some part of it. Having a scoop of it on your plate, even just a small scoop, allowed you to partake in the beauty. I'm sure she brought salads because she had probably noticed that there was not one vegetable to be found in our entire house, unless you consider Pork & Beans a vegetable.

Mama used to complain how Aunt Winnie "always comes to eat, but it never crosses her mind to bring anything." I never understood this, but I didn't dare argue with her. I can count on one hand the times I chose to openly contradict my mama, and it did not turn out well. By the time I had reached puberty, I learned to turn my face and slip away into apathy. Numbness was a great friend of mine. I honestly do not know how I was saved from the sort of thing John suffers from. But, no doubt, God spared me for some reason, and he gave it to John as a cross for some reason. For some reason. I don't use this phrase to mean I am mystified and questioning. I use it literally. It is all that it is for some reason. On the days when he is not suffering it, John would agree. In fact, he has said as much. One thing that is bound to save him is his hope. On days when he is not feeling hopeless, he possesses a good amount of hope.

Maybe there is something genetic to it all. I am thinking now of Jolene. She is Terry and Jimmy's biological mother, and she lived a highly dysfunctional life and died depressed. It might have skipped a generation, and then again maybe not. Maybe Terry just has the skills to deal with it. There was a time in her life when she went numb. She speaks of it sometimes. She credits Lily with lifting her from the mire and saving her marriage. I wish Lily were still alive for John. I do suspect he grieves her loss even still. What John and Lily had was special. Not at all reproducible. It is gone.

I know from experience, sometimes gone things are more painful than non-existent things. I look with sadness on my past happiness with John. Sometimes I wish I had never had it. What was the purpose of it? Only to show me what can be had and lost. Had I never had it, misery wouldn't be so miserable. I wouldn't know what to long for. I could just be happy without happiness. Now, all I have is a memory of happiness, and it makes me appreciate the strength of old people. The ones who still manage a smile when everything and everyone they hold dear has gone away. I hope for those kind of heroics, for the sake of this baby who needs a smiling mother.

John has made the coffee particularly strong this morning, and I am grateful. If I am going to drink decaf, it's got to have some flavor. Nothing else has changed around here since I told John about the baby. Maybe I didn't really tell him? Maybe it was a dream? But I am drinking decaf. So he must know. These are the ridiculous thoughts I entertain as he sits across from me reading the news.

"This mug has a crack in it," I say. "I'm afraid it's going to start leaking."

"Let me see." He takes the mug from my hand. "There's no crack. What makes you think there's a crack?"

"I can tell by the sound when I flick it. It thuds instead of tings."

"It'll be OK." He hands the cup back to me.

"Well, maybe it will. For now. But this will probably be the last time we use it. It's going to leak any minute."

"There's no possible way you could know that."

"There's a hairline fracture in the ceramic somewhere. You just can't see it. Or won't."

"What do you mean, 'or won't?' I looked. There's nothing there."

"Maybe you didn't look closely enough."

"OK," he sighs and takes the cup out of my hand again. A drop of something warm and wet hits my toe.

"Ugh, there you go," I say. "It's leaking."

"Oh, you're right," he says without expression. "It is. Shoot." I hear the clink against the porcelain as he sets the mug in the sink.

"See?" I say. "Sometimes the blind can see better than the sighted."

"Is that a quote? Sounds like something Jesus would say."

"Thank you. That's quite a compliment. I think I made it up. But I don't know. Maybe it is from the Bible."

"Or a fortune cookie."

"Anyhow, is there another cup of coffee in my future?"

"Sure, I can get you one. But if you're so capable, why

don't you ever get your own coffee?"

There was a time when John would never have dreamed of saying something like that to me. I happen to know he found delight in serving me, which is why I never felt like a burden.

"Don't take that the wrong way," he says. "I'm more than happy to get it for you. I'm sorry Charlotte. That didn't come out right."

"No, that's OK. I should be getting the coffee. Would you like a cup?"

"No Charlotte. I don't want you to wait on me."

"Why not? You've been waiting on me for years. And I know you can't always be happy about it. But you never complain. And that's what makes you a saint."

"You've got to be kidding. A saint."

"Nope not kidding." I take four or five long, smooth sips. The coffee is good. John always gets it exactly the way I like it. Perfect amount of cream. I am not so sure I could do that for him every morning. I'd get it right sometimes. Maybe even frequently. But he gets it right always.

"Now that I think about it, that fork in our drawer could not have come from Aunt Winnie's salad," I say, not planning for my thoughts to materialize outside my head.

"Hmmm?"

"Oh, nothing."

It was just a regular dinner-sized fork, not the very large kind you would bring for a salad bowl. Anyway, I would find that fork in the drawer and I would find comfort in it. Was it the mere reminder of my aunt and all her colors or was it the thought that she would have to come back for it or we would have to make it a point to see her again in order to return it? Then, again, I wouldn't have wanted to return it. I used it as often as I could, whenever someone else hadn't mindlessly grabbed it. I ate mostly things like fried eggs, Spam and Pork & Beans with it. Though there was never any salad on my plate for those 363 days a year when Aunt Winnie was not around, it reminded me of the deep and bright greens of romaine mixed with spinach, which served as the backdrop for the bright red pops of cherry tomatoes and black olives, oranges and yellows of bell peppers, purple and almost purples of onions and radishes, the white jicama and earthen-colored mushrooms thrown in for contrast, tossed in a clear glass, elliptical bowl, like none I had ever seen before or since.

Something about those vegetables and fabrics and earrings that my aunt brought into my life twice a year made me want to travel, made me want to learn. They made me to understand there was something beyond the colorless places I had known. Salad and cheap gewgaws might very well be the reason I decided to backpack across Europe after high school (financed by my aunt) and then pursue a degree in art history (financed by student loans I've yet to fully pay off). I am quite certain no other child from my trailer park chose this path, especially the ones who were going blind. But I figured if I was going to lose my sight, I had better take it all in while I could. And I have absolutely no regrets about that. Seeing a fuzzy, out of focus Eiffel Tower right before you beats seeing a high-res picture of it any day. The smells and sound and tastes of Paris might even be better than the sights anyway. I know all the culinary experts say you eat with your eyes, but no one has to see a French pastry to understand how glorious it is.

Yes, I learned a great many things from Aunt Winnie, though there were only two things she overtly taught me: 1. Vegetables are a necessary part of my diet and 2. God loves me without measure.

She was probably one of the main reasons I became Catholic. In my childhood, I didn't know any other Catholics besides her. She converted when she married her husband, who died young from liver cancer. When I went backpacking in Europe I found myself on the Way of St. James in Spain, visiting all the holy sites. I had met a fellow pilgrim and we unintentionally travelled together for awhile. I say "unintentionally" because that's how it is on the Way. You just walk and everyone else just walks and sometimes you end up walking together. This fellow happened to be a Catholic priest. I had deeper conversations with him than I ever had in my life. And I came away with more questions than I'd ever had in my life. So when I got home from Europe, I caught a bus to the closest Catholic church and enrolled in RCIA classes. I came into the Church the following Easter.

I would love to know where Aunt Winnie's fork got to. I really doubt it ever got returned. I wonder if one of my sisters has it now. I took next to nothing from the house when mama died. My two sisters divided pretty much everything. I wish now I had looked for that fork. It had a shell on the handle. I have never thought of this until now, but that fork might have been prophetic. The shell happens to be the symbol for the Way of St. James.

16

Protocol Violation

I decided I should try to see my Daddy before it is too late. But it is too late. I don't know why I hadn't considered the possibility that my father could be dead. I called my sisters to tell them. They already knew. He passed away three years ago. They never bothered to notify me. But that is typical of my family. The last I heard from them was when I invited them to come to Mass to celebrate with me my entry into the Church. They had prior commitments. The next time I contacted them was to give them an update on my eyes. I don't know why I did that. I really didn't want to tell them how bad my vision had gotten, but I guess I just felt like somebody in my family should know, though the last thing I wanted was pity, so I was relieved when I never heard back from them.

I remember as a kid, sitting in my late Uncle Jim's wheelchair when we had our family reunions. My aunt kept the chair in her bedroom, maybe thinking she would use it herself one day. When she had a full house, she'd wheel it out to give us extra seating. I always felt uncomfortable if I had to be the one to sit in it. I felt like people would feel sorry for me, even though they knew it was just a place to sit and my legs were perfectly fine. That feeling returned to me the moment I heard the diagnosis, three days shy of my fifteenth birthday. I longed to be invisible. After getting over the shock, though, I tried to find the bright side. Yes, I actually thought there would be one. I thought this because I was not fully aware how messed up my family really was. I actually thought that they would start to be nice to me if I were disabled. They, in fact, treated me no differently than they always had. I guess they were probably the least discriminatory people you ever want to meet. They treated that conversation with the doctor that day like it never happened. There were some times when I wondered if it really had. Maybe I had dreamed it all, though I did find myself able to see less and less.

"Maybe we can take a trip and visit your daddy's grave," John says as he merges onto the freeway.

"Nah. If I didn't see him when he was alive, there's no use going now that he's dead," I say.

If it wasn't for the fact that I can't drive myself, I wonder if John would even accompany me to these doctors' appointments. Aside from his occasional hints that we are not the ideal parents, he has been virtually silent on the coming of this child. He says he's going to buy a crib and set it up in our room, but he hasn't gotten around to it yet. He says he will take me shopping for baby clothes and blankets and diapers, but there's always some reason not to go. He rarely has questions for the doctor. It's almost as if he thinks the baby is going to somehow go away.

"We have a few minutes to spare, Charlotte. Do you mind if we make a stop?"

"No, not at all. Where are we stopping?"

"I want to show you something."

"What?"

"You'll see."

He parks the car and comes to the passenger side to get me. He puts my hand into the crook of his arm, as he always does, and leads me to some sort of courtyard, from what I can tell. My vision is particularly bad today because yesterday was my monthly eye drop treatment, which is supposed to help in the long-range, but temporarily makes things worse. "Where are we?"

"Here," he says, placing my hand on something stone and spherical. "Look at this."

My hand moves over the object, which is the size of a person's head and then around to the front of it. I feel a nose, eyes and wrinkles. Lots of wrinkles in the face. And a smile. John guides my hand down over the arm and I feel another face—a small one, a baby's face. He is also smiling. She is holding him and they are smiling at each other.

"Hmmm," I say.

"What?"

"Well. It's beautiful. But why did the sculptor make the Blessed Mother so old?"

"It's not the Blessed Mother. It's Mother Teresa."

"Mother Teresa?"

"I came here the other day because I just happened to be driving by this parish. And I remembered I had my rosary in my pocket and I decided I would go inside the church and pray. And I found her here. Holding this little baby. And the oddest thing was that someone had draped a rosary over her fingers, and the rosary was exactly like mine. A cheap blue plastic rosary."

"Wow."

"Yeah, and there's something else. I don't know if it's my imagination or not."

"What?"

He takes my hand and guides it to the baby's face.

"Feel the eyes, Charlotte."

"Beautiful sculpture."

"Do the eyes seem different to you in any way?"

"I don't know. Different how?"

"Here, Charlotte. Here, have a seat." John takes me by the arm and walks me to a bench. I wish I could see this place. It seems so lovely and peaceful.

"I will tell you, Charlotte. I will tell you what I owe it to you to tell you." I hear him swallow hard. "When I was in my teens, I had finally gotten myself a group of friends. I hadn't had a group before. You know, I'd had a friend here or there, but I hadn't really belonged anywhere. One of them invited me along to a movie once after I helped him out with a biology test, and suddenly I was in. Soon, they started hanging out at our house. You know, our house was always the best place to hang out. The best food. The best stuff to do. My mom planned it that way. But there was just one problem."

"What?"

"Lily."

"Lily was a problem?"

"Yes, she was a problem because I was a weak and shallow kid."

"What do you mean?"

"There came a moment, when one of these friends thought it would be OK to make fun of Lily. He waited until she left the room and then he said something very crude about her and Frank being together. The rest of the guys laughed, and then they looked at me, probably waiting to see if I was going to get mad. I just stared at the screen, pretending to be engrossed in my video game. So it became this ongoing, running joke every time they came over."

"You never said anything?"

"At first, no. Then came that awful moment when I joined in. As soon as the comment left my mouth, I felt horrible. I felt like dirt all that night. I wanted to get up the strength to tell them that I was wrong and they've been wrong, making fun of Lily and something so private. But I never did. I just started suggesting we go somewhere else to hang out. You know, kind of subtly, so they wouldn't know I was upset about anything. But our house really had the best setup for fun and food, so they always wanted to come back."

"Did Lily ever know?"

"No. It's an odd thing too. Nobody ever kept secrets from Lily or talked behind her back. As a matter of fact, there were conversations you could have around and with Lily that you couldn't have with anyone else in the room. Mom and Uncle Jimmy used to take her with them into the confessional when she was little. When someone had to have a private conversation with someone, everyone was asked to leave except Lily. When I had to tell my mom or dad something, I certainly wouldn't have wanted Beth or Laura or even Katie in the room. But Lily was OK. So she probably knew a lot more than the rest of us. And there was never any risk involved in that. So now I live with the knowledge that I betrayed her. It actually makes me feel physically sick to my stomach."

"What triggers that guilt? Because there are times you go through your life without being hounded."

"I don't know. I think that's the chemical part. Whatever my brain chemistry is going to do, it's going to do. But it uses my remorse as a weapon against me. And I don't see how it will ever change. It's in the past and there's no way to go back and make peace with something that ugly."

"But you are focusing on this one ugly thing. Ninety-nine

percent of what you had with Lily was beautiful. You have so many wonderful memories."

"I have too many memories of Lily. And every time I have a memory, it is tainted by remorse. Sometimes I'm able to beat it down by quickly shifting my focus away from Lily. Other times, I just relive it in my head. Or make up alternate endings in my mind—the way things should have turned out."

"We all have a large collection of alternate endings. They are kind of useless without a time machine."

"Oh, if only I could get access to one of those."

"So what did finally happen with your friends?"

"They eventually stopped making fun of Lily."

"Did you end up telling them off?"

"No, regretfully, it wasn't me. A new guy had been brought into the group one day, a friend of someone's. When he heard the crude comments toward Lily, he stood up and told them off. In a nice way, he just said, you know something like, 'hey guys, that's really not cool.'"

"And that's all it took?"

"That's all it took."

"Wow, I had no idea it took so little to make those kinds of bullies back down."

"I know, I was surprised by that too. And I wondered, and still do, why couldn't I have done just that little bit? I'm the one who loved Lily, and I didn't come to her defense. You can't know what she meant to me when I was a kid. I had great parents, but Lily offered pure, unmitigated joy. She didn't expect anything of me. She just loved me."

"So, see? Asking her forgiveness would have been pointless. You know she would have forgiven you, and you saved her from hurt feelings. My aunt Winnie used to say, 'What you don't know can't hurt ya.'"

"Oh, I'm sure all her life she thought I would have gone to the matt to defend her. She never suffered any insecurities over whether people loved her. Probably because she knew how to love. It probably never crossed her mind that other people don't."

"You loved her, John. You know you did."

"I can picture myself stepping in front of a moving truck to save her. I would have laid down my life for her. No question. In my mind. But in real life, I wasn't even able to lose a few friends for her."

"So what ever happened to that kid who stuck up for Lily?"

"He died in a car accident."

"It was Eddie?"

"It was Eddie."

I put my arm around John's waist and lay my head on his shoulder. He strokes my hair.

"I was working up the nerve to tell her what I'd done, but I never could. When she had her stroke, I prayed and prayed she would come back to us so I could beg her to forgive me."

"But you didn't hurt her, John. She had no idea what those kids were saying."

"Not exactly. But there were always those moments when she would come into the room and all the talking would stop and the grins and silent snickers would start. You know how kids are. And Lily was intuitive. On some level, I feel like she knew something she could never put her finger on. I wanted to tell her she wasn't crazy and that I was a creep for hanging out with those kids. There were plenty of kids at my school who liked people with disabilities, even went out of their way to befriend them. But I had my mind made up I was going to try to get into this certain clique of cool kids and I sacrificed all that I believed in to be one of them. I even ended up with a really beautiful and popular girlfriend, and I didn't want to rock the boat and risk ticking anyone off with my defense of Lily. I'm sure Lily wondered why I didn't want to be around her anymore. I was too busy with all the cool people. Found out eventually, the hard way, that cool people can be pretty cold."

"But you did more than enough to make it up to her, John. Weren't you always there for her towards the end of her life?

"Well, I tried to make it up to her. But how do you make up for lost time when it comes to love? She died when I was twenty, and I should have twenty years of love to show for it. As it was, I lost a good two years of that, and there's no way to get those back. They are just two loveless years. Like a two-year blackout. Like it all went dark."

ಏ⚬ꂚꂷꂚꂷꂚꂷꂚꂷꂚꂷ

My chest feels heavy, pressed full with love, as I imagine the tiny human being floating on the screen. There's an entire person within me. The more I think about it, the more I labor to grasp the truth all humanity has taken for granted since the beginning of time. Women have babies. I have known how that works since I was three. But the fact that a human being can live inside another human being seems like fiction. A fable. A beautiful fable, but a fable nonetheless. How did God think that up? I mean, what did the angels think when He told them? Did He put it something like this? *They will carry each other within themselves. And from this, they will learn what it means to love.*

"OK," the ultrasound tech says. "I think I've got what I need. I'd like to have doctor come in and give it a look, so if you wouldn't mind just hanging out here."

"What is it?" I ask. "Do you see something wrong?"

"Don't worry. The baby is fine. The doctor will be able to discuss it with you."

"It's the neck," John says. "Isn't it?" His voice cracks, as if he might be choking back tears.

"The neck?" I say, sitting up. "What about the neck? What's wrong?"

"The neck is thick," John says. I am confused because I had no idea he knew how to read ultrasounds.

"Let me go get the doctor," the tech says. "Just relax. The baby is fine. You'll see. Everything will be fine."

As soon as the door closes, I grab both of John's arms and pull him, so I can get my face close to his. But I can't see his eyes. "What is it John? What did you see?"

"I didn't see anything, Honey. I'm sorry. I didn't mean to say it that way and get you all upset."

"But you said the neck is thick."

"I was just guessing."

"Guessing? How does somebody guess something like that?"

The door opens.

"Hello, I'm Dr. LaRoy." I hear the stool roll and then stop and then creak, so I assume he is straddling and sitting as doctors do. "Let's have a peak at this little one."

I can tell by John's irregular breathing that he is crying.

"Well, there's no need to be alarmed," the doctor says. "We're just going to have a look here."

"No, It's OK," John sniffs. "I'm not alarmed."

There is silence in the room for a few minutes as the wand moves over my belly and then the doctor says, "OK then. I think I got a good glimpse. Let me have a quick look at your chart and then I'll be right back with you. You can get dressed." The door closes.

I grope for my blouse. Normally John would be holding it for me, so I can slide my arms into the sleeves. But I can hear him pulling tissues from a box.

"What did you see, John?" I ask wrestling with my shirt. "What's going on."

"I didn't see anything, Charlotte. I'm not sure what's going on."

"Why are you so upset?"

"I'm not upset."

"You sure sound upset."

"No, I—"

A knock at the door.

"Me again," the doctor says.

He sits and straddles again. "OK, so it looks like you two are the parents of a special baby."

"We are?" I say. "What does that mean?"

"This is the point in our conversation, according to the protocol of this institution, when I am supposed to write you a referral. But I don't do that because I happen to know a number of people just like your baby, and I wouldn't wish any of them away."

I can hear John sobbing now. I wish he would stop. I feel my hands start to shake. Plus, I am embarrassed for him.

"Your baby has Down syndrome."

"Down syndrome?" My voice sounds faint inside my head. "How is that possible?"

"Well, it's not what you would call common," the doctor says. "But it does happen. Trisomy 21 is the most frequent chromosomal abnormality."

"No, I know that," I say. "I just mean—" I can't finish because I can't explain my question. I guess what I would ask is, what are the chances of a woman who marries a man whose aunt had down syndrome and whose cousin, who was supposed to have Down syndrome but doesn't, adopts a child with Down syndrome and brings the child for a recent visit—what would be the chances of that woman's baby having Down syndrome? In other words, why all this Down syndrome? *Do you know, Lily? What's this all about?*

Lily is silent on the matter. She is pensive perhaps. Or she wants to let me figure it out on my own.

৪৩❀ᲝᲐ

17

Things Unknown to Lily

The car ride is excruciating. John hasn't said a word since we left the doctor's office. I don't know what I'm going to do. This probably couldn't happen to a more ill-equipped couple. I know John must be thinking the same thing. The silence is killing me. But I am not going to break it. I don't want to hear what he might have to say on this topic. I have heard of men pressuring their wives to terminate. I know John wouldn't do that. Thank God I know that. This is hard, but it's not as hard as it could be. Lily will make it easier. At least I hope so. I guess it could work the opposite way. John knows exactly what we're in for. And it won't be easy given my blindness. Not easy, but possible. I hope John sees that. I hope he sees it as possible.

"Do you want to live in Boston or Seattle?"

That is the question that breaks the interminable silence. His voice is calm. Almost genial.

"Boston or Seattle?" I ask "We're moving?"

"We will need the help of family. We can't do this alone."

"No. You're right," I say. "We can't."

I try to control the smile that is forcing its way across my face and the tears that want to pour.

"I talked to Lily," he says.

"You did?"

"Yes. I told her about the baby."

"I'll bet she was pleased."

"She already knew."

"She did?"

"Yeah."

"So, she knew about the Down syndrome too?"

"Oh, yes. She knew. She knew I wanted a second chance. I *need* a second chance. I'm going to do it right this time. I'm going to figure out how to do it. How to love. Not just how to *feel* love. But how to *really* love."

He pulls into a parking lot, puts the car in park, takes off his seat belt and hugs me tight to him, like I haven't been hugged in a million years.

"Oh, Charlotte, I hope you can help me. I know you can. You know the secret, don't you? You know how to love."

It is one of those millionth-year hugs, yes. And it feels like heaven is at my door. And I am unable to murmur a single word.

"I'm not exactly sure how it all works up there, Charlotte. But I told Lily I'd do anything for a second chance, even though I knew it was impossible. And somehow she arranged for it. I prayed and I asked all of heaven, if there was any way I could have another shot at being good to someone like Lily. I didn't think there was. I didn't think there was a way. I never imagined this, Charlotte. "

All I can manage is a soft whisper under my breath. *Thank you, Lily.*

John releases me from his embrace and puts the car in drive. "I can't wait to love this baby, Charlotte. His life will not be easy. But what we have to do is easy. We just have to love him."

"I am very lucky to be married to a man like you, John. So many men would say this is too hard. Too hard to be the parent. And too hard to be the child."

He shifts the car back into park.

"Lily's life was hard," he says. "I never understood that. Why it had to be so hard."

"Really? I always thought she loved life."

"She did. She loved it because she didn't know an easier way. Much in the same way that people loved life before the internet, and now we're miserable for even one moment without it. She didn't know how hard her life was. The sheer difficulty of her life—the imperfection of her existence—those were among the things unknown to Lily."

"So she was happy."

"Exceedingly so. In the vast majority of moments. Yes."

"So how is that a handicap? Wouldn't you rather be happy than informed?"

"I would rather be happy than any other thing in the world."

I don't know why that answer surprises me. Why am I expecting something different?

"Wouldn't you?" he asks. "It's what we all want, isn't it?"

"Ah, yes. Indeed it is."

"Charlotte?" He takes me by the shoulders and looks closely into my face. "You know that Mother Teresa statue I showed you?"

"Yeah?"

"Well, the baby she is holding, I wasn't certain at first, but now I know. I know for sure."

"The eyes!"

"Yes! The eyes, Charlotte! The baby has Down syndrome."

He puts the car in drive, puts his seat belt back on and

drifts to the road. A few minutes pass in silence. I, for sure, am smiling, and I imagine John is too.

"Oh, look," he says. "Basil's. I'm starving. How about you? You want to get a bite?"

"Yes, starving. I really want a banana split right now. With peanut butter and sunflower seeds. I know that's crazy. But that's what I want. With Captain Crunch ground up and sprinkled over the top. And a dollop of sour cherry jelly."

"Don't know where we're going to find a restaurant that serves that. Looks like we're going to the grocery store."

"Sorry."

"Don't worry. Your baby cravings are no worse than the strange things you Southerners normally eat."

"What do you mean?"

"Wonder bread, spread with applesauce with milk poured over it?"

"It's a culinary delight. But what about your cracker soup? You can't tell me crackers laid out in a boil with coffee poured over them and sugar sprinkled on top isn't just a little unusual."

"That one came from the Italian neighbor my mother had when she was growing up. It had been passed down through the generations from the first immigrants, who had nothing in their cupboard but some saltines and some Maxwell House. But you need to try it. It makes a flavor all its own, unlike anything you've ever tasted."

"Same with applesauce, bread and milk. Ain't nothing like it. It's the lazy man's apple pie ala mode."

I always feel like I slip into a heavy southern drawl when I talk about food. All the words come out the way my mama used to say them.

"Actually, you know what I want even more than a banana split with peanut butter, sprinkled with sunflower seeds and

Captain Crunch?" I ask.

"Don't forget the dollop of sour cherry jelly."

"Ah yes, the dollop. But even more than that, I have a different sort of craving."

"For what? Just name it?"

"We haven't been to Communion for so long, John. And I really need it. And I need to go to confession first."

"Sure, Charlotte. Sure."

"Can we go now?"

"Two fifty-eight on a Friday. I don't know, Charlotte. I doubt there are any confessions going on now."

"Remember when you were able to find Lily a priest just by driving around?"

"Yeah, for two hours."

"I mean, I know you're hungry, John. But—oh John. I have this other little person growing inside me, you know? I wonder."

"Wonder what?"

"You know how mothers and babies in the womb share the same food? Will our baby receive Jesus when I receive Communion?"

"Wow. Is that how it works?"

"I don't know. Let's ask the confessor when we find him."

"OK." He has a smile in his voice. "We'll drive. As far as it takes, Charlotte. We will drive to Kalamazoo if we have to. I don't mind."

I close my eyes and let my head fall back on the headrest. In my mind, I am walking a stroller along a tree-lined path. The sunlight dances through the leaves all around me. The colors are vivid, like I've never seen before. It is a pram-style stroller, like the English ladies once used, so the baby is facing toward me. I can't see his face, though I have a deep longing to know every detail about it.

"So you never answered my question," John says. "Boston or Seattle?"

The sun doesn't shine much in Seattle. Not so much in Boston either. I will miss the light on my face and the dry sidewalk under my feet.

"Anywhere," I say. "Anywhere you want to go, John."

☍✂☃

About the Author

Since entering the field of fiction in 2011, former newspaper reporter Sherry Boas has released seven novels, including five in the beloved Lily series. Although she won numerous awards in her ten-year career as a journalist for a daily newspaper, it was her vocation as a mother that would best prepare her for an author's career. For her, truth resounds and inspiration abounds in the struggles and triumphs of every-day family life. In awed wonder, the Boases have watched a number of miracles unfold in their faith-filled and often-zany Arizona home. Sherry and her husband Phil are the grateful adoptive parents of four children, including one with Down syndrome and another who was born fifteen weeks early.

In stolen moments between home schooling, burning dinner and mating mismatched socks, Sherry runs Caritas Press from her home office, which looks more like animal shelter meets Lego factory than it does publishing house. If there are any typos in the final product, blame the mind-numbing racket of the hamster running relentlessly in his wheel or the yipping Chihuahua keeping the howling husky in line. The children, of course, observe perfect silence all day long.

In addition to Catholic fiction, Caritas Press publishes a series of rosary meditations for moms, dads, children, teens, grandparents and altar servers and an expanding line of Catholic and pro-life children's books including *Victoria's Sparrows, Miraculous Me, Barnyard Bliss* and *God's Easter Gifts*.

In 2014, Sherry made her debut into youth fiction with *Billowtail*, a novel that chronicles the adventures of a band of squirrels on the Way of St. James in Medieval Spain. Her first children's picture book *Little Maximus Myers* (Tau Publishing), tells the tale of an altar boy too small to carry the cross who comes to understand that our limitations can bring us closer to Christ.

Sherry is also author of *A Mother's Bouquet: Rosary Meditations for Moms* and the novel, *Wing Tip*, a unique tale of relentless love about a priest whose mother's deathbed confession reveals a shocking family secret.

You can find Sherry's work in Catholic bookstores nationwide, at LilyTrilogy.com, CaritasPress.org and CatholicWord.com and in a jumble of cardboard boxes in the closet under her stairs.

Fiction by Sherry Boas

  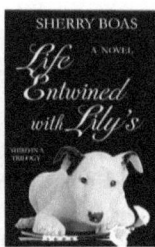  

The transforming power of love is at the heart of this poignant series about the people whose lives are moved by a woman with Down syndrome. Lily's story is told with such brutal yet touching honesty, it will have you laughing one minute and reduced to tears the next.

Until Lily
Wherever Lily Goes
Life Entwined with Lily's
The Things Lily Knew
Things Unknown to Lily

"...You will be entranced, you will experience the joys and sorrows of the characters, you will cry, and you will not be able to put Lily down."
– Dr. Jeff Mirus of CatholicCulture.org

Wing Tip

Dante De Luz's steel was forged in his youth, in the crucible of harsh losses and triumphant love. But that steel gets tested like never before as the revelation of a family secret presents the young Catholic priest with the toughest challenge of his life, with stakes that couldn't get any higher.

"Sure to be a Catholic Classic"
"Magnificent read"

Robert Curtis, Catholic Sun

CatholicWord.com   CaritasPress.org

Children's Books by Sherry Boas

It is the year 1214. A baby squirrel falls from the nest and lands in the passing saddlebag of a 13-year-old boy. Still blind, deaf, hairless and unable to eat solid food, there is little hope for Puttermunch's survival. Moved by the persistent pleading of his distraught mother, a selection of five squirrels set out to find Puttermunch, launching a perilous and life-altering journey on the Way of St. James in Spain. The road is fraught with failure for Billowtail, Tippy, Nip, Sugarcoat and Sir Sniff, until these well-meaning tree squirrels, born to be loners and hoarders, learn the value of community and self-sacrifice.

"A delightful story that quickly captures the reader's interest, sparks the imagination, and, without being preachy, leads one to a deeper sense of the mystery of creation. I recommend it for kids and adults."
The Most Reverend Thomas J. Olmsted
Bishop of Phoenix

Little Maximus Myers never liked being little, until one day, while carrying the cross in the procession at Mass, he discovered how our weaknesses can bring us closer to Christ. Inspired by real-life events of her own children, acclaimed author Sherry Boas weaves a story that will delight and inspire not only altar servers, but all who wish to give their best to Christ despite their own limitations.

Things are usually perfect at Grandma and Grandpa's cabin. But not on the day after a fierce storm comes to Fossil Lake. The cellar, stocked with all the food the family needs, is blocked by a fallen tree. The bridge is washed out, and there's no way to get to town. But it isn't her own rumbling tummy that worries Victoria as much as the sparrows' broken and empty bird feeder. Before the day is through, the young girl will come to understand what providence is all about.

CatholicWord.com   CaritasPress.org

Children's Titles from Caritas Press

What thoughts crossed your mother's mind the first time she laid eyes on you? What dreams did your father hold in his heart? This delightful story by Ruth Pendergast Sissel is told from the perspective of a baby in the womb, listening to his parents' awe at seeing him on ultrasound for the first time.

The animals can't wait to share the news, Something exciting and beautiful has come to be! A new baby enters the world! all of creation rejoices as word of Mr. And Mrs. Hoot's owlet spreads throughout the farm.

With unbridled joy, their voices rise. All things old, become refreshed Welcome Babe! A joyous day! We pray your life be blessed!

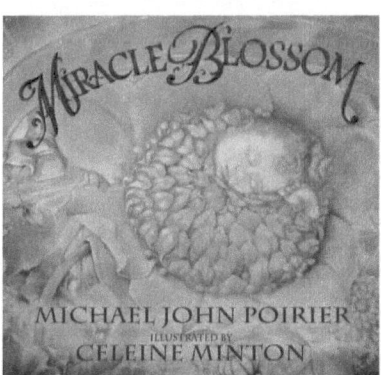

What happens when something unexpected begins to grow in the pathway, ruining the design of your beautiful garden? Miracle Blossom will inspire in you a new way of looking at life, in all its unplanned splendor. Paired with the music of beloved singer/songwriter Michael John Poirier, a gift to you on MP3, this pro-life story aims to lift a child's mind and heart to heaven, with its stunning illustrations by gifted and insightful artist Celeine Minton. Endorsed by theology professor and author Dr. Scott Hahn.

Bella and Pablo love Easter egg hunts. So many wonderful goodies just waiting to be found inside each egg! But the brother and sister are about to discover there's much more to Easter than candy and toys, as they embark on a very special Easter egg hunt that will reveal all of God's greatest gifts to us.

CatholicWord.com   CaritasPress.org

Rosary Meditations from Caritas Press

A MOTHER'S BOUQUET: ROSARY MEDITATIONS FOR MOMS

Straight from the heart of a mother, these rosary meditations for moms will uplift and sanctify your journey. Sherry Boas, author of the critically acclaimed Lily Trilogy, offers these prayers in hopes that moms will grow in holiness and come to more fully treasure the wondrous vocation of motherhood enfolded in the mysteries of Christ's life, death and resurrection. **By Sherry Boas**

A FATHER'S HEART: ROSARY MEDITATIONS FOR DADS

Discover the heart of true fatherhood as it relates to the life, death and resurrection of Christ. With pearls of wisdom and glimpses into the eternal and relentless love of God, Father Doug Lorig draws on his own experiences as a father and pastor to bring parents to a deeper understanding of their role in God's perfect plan of salvation. Grow in holiness within the wondrous vocation of fatherhood as you pray these rosary written especially for dads. **By Father Doug Lorig**

GENERATIONS OF LOVE: ROSARY MEDITATIONS FOR GRANDPARENTS

Get a glimpse into the heavenly realities of grandparenthood as you come to understand the beautiful and invaluable role you play as parents of parents. Through these insightful and uplifting meditations, Author Anne Belle-Oudry reminds us that, while grandchildren are undoubtedly among life's richest rewards, grandparents, too, are an inestimable blessing to their families as they strive to lead their loved ones closer to Christ through their prayers, example and unconditional love. **By Anne Belle-Oudry**

A CHILD'S TREASURE: ROSARY MEDITATIONS FOR CHILDREN

Grow to love the Lord more deeply through these meditations written by children for children. With insight into how Mother Mary loves Jesus, authors Derek Rebello, Elsa Schiavone and Michael Boas show us how to follow Him more closely in our everyday lives and discover that our faith is truly our greatest treasure. **By Derek Rebello, Elsa Schiavone and Michael Boas**

AMAZING LOVE: ROSARY MEDITATIONS FOR TEENS

Grow to understand the unsurpassed importance of your friendship with Jesus through these rosary meditations written by teens for teens. Authors Mari Seaberg, Adrian Inclan and Maria Boas show how the passion, death and resurrection of Christ sustain our lives today as we strive to do His will in the face of a multitude of decisions, illuminated by his amazing love. **By Adrian Inclan, Mari Seaberg and Maria Boas**

A SERVANT'S HEART: ROSARY MEDITATIONS FOR ALTAR SERVERS

Prepare your heart for true service with these Meditations written especially for altar servers. Reflect on the meaning of your calling as it relates to the mysteries of Christ's life, death and resurrection and as it applies to your own life in a world that is often at odds with the message of Christ's self-sacrificing love. **By Peter Troiano**

CatholicWord.com   CaritasPress.org

www.ingramcontent.com/pod-product-compliance
Lightning Source LLC
Chambersburg PA
CBHW052140170626
46812CB00004B/1517